3.50

THE GREYLING

THE GREYLING

BY

DAPHNE ROOKE

REYNAL & COMPANY, NEW YORK

*The characters in this book
are fictitious*

CHARACTERS

THE DELPORTS, PIETER (called the OUBAAS) and his wife TANT BERTHA. MAARTEN, their twenty-two year old son, called BASIE. The Delports live at their farm, Diamant, seven miles from Perelkop. They have diamond diggings at Jakkalspan.

ILSE VAN DOORN, the narrator. Mrs. Van Doorn lives with her small son, RAYMOND, near the Delports at Perelkop. Her husband is serving a term in prison.

BOKKIE SIPHO, called THE GREYLING, young Coloured girl, working for the Delports.

THE ROTTCHERS, the local power in Perelkop. Rottcher is organizer of the Veld Guard; his wife is the social force.

LUKE, Mrs. Van Doorn's overseer, Coloured.

SIPHO, a Native working for the Delports; Bokkie's grandfather.

BRUGGEMANN, and his wife CISSIE, neighbours to the Delports at the diggings. They join the Delports at Diamant to help build the church.

PETRUS KOTZE, the evangelist.

CHAPTER 1

I was at my place in Perelkop when the Prime Minister was shot in Johannesburg. The Delports were on their claim at Jakkalspan diamond diggings. They heard the news from their Coloured servant whom they usually called the Greyling: her name was Bokkie Sipho. She had been listening in secret to a transistor radio owned by the son Maarten. The Oubaas and Tant Bertha, as the Delports were known, were on their way across the claim to visit some friends at the other end of the diggings.

They turned at the sound of Bokkie's racing footsteps.

"I suppose she is coming to ask for permission to go to Jakkalspan," said Tante, indulgently: Bokkie had changed into her best dress and silk stockings the moment Tante's back was turned. "Can you blame her for wanting to show herself off, she's getting to be pretty, not so? What would some White girls give for such teeth and fine skin and such a small waist . . ."

Then Bokkie gasped out: "It was on the radio. Someone has shot him, someone shot the Prime Minister, nonna, my baas."

The first thing they thought to do was to pray and Tante looked to the Oubaas to lead them, so with a voice of thunder he started them on the Psalm which begins: Hear my cry, O God. . . . Tante had on her best black dress and the Oubaas was wearing his suit for they had intended to go on later to a meeting held by the evangelist Petrus Kotze; some people passing thought that they were members of a religious sect and stopped to watch them. Oubaas and Tante stood but the Greyling was kneeling in the dust and throughout the Psalm went on shrieking: "God, they've shot him, O God, he's finished . . ." and suddenly flew up and away skimming across the humped land, calling, yelling, her voice now shrill now deep like an organ, and her legs in a paroxysm: behind her the dust was laid by her water.

"She's lying," sobbed Tante. "The Greyling was always a liar."

"She's drunk," said the Oubaas.

The people who had mistaken the Delports for members of a religious sect realized that they were wrong. They thought now that Tante and the Oubaas had something to do with a funeral because she was in her black dress and he in his suit.

"Excuse me," said one of the men. "Is there anything we can do to help? Is it a bereavement?"

"Then you have heard nothing?" said the Oubaas in relief. "That creature of ours has just told us that the Prime Minister is wounded."

"It's Communists' talk," shouted a woman.

8

"The maid says she heard it on the radio," said Tante.

"Let us go and hear for ourselves."

They turned back to go to the Delports' tent. The evangelist Petrus Kotze was riding towards them on his motor-bike, a figure shooting right out of the cloudless sky. He sped along the straight road and would have passed them with a wave of his hand but the Oubaas yelled to him to stop.

"We have heard such terrible news, Petrus," said the Oubaas, high above the roaring of the engine. "They say the Prime Minister has been shot."

Petrus was silent but only while he thought of a quotation: "Keep me as the apple of the eye, hide me under the shadow of thy wings, from the wicked that oppress me, from my deadly enemies, who compass me about." The women looked at him admiringly: his knowledge of the Psalms was phenomenal, in fact he had memorized them all, as well as several books in the old Testament.

"You have heard nothing about it?" Oubaas asked.

"I've been in the veld meditating."

"Do you think it is true?" Tante asked him.

Petrus nodded and opened his mouth. He knew also by heart the lamentations of Jeremiah, and as he was fond of reciting these, Oubaas said hurriedly: "We're going to listen-in on the radio. Come too, Petrus," then led the way down the road with Petrus chugging along behind on the bike.

The radio was still playing softly as the Greyling had left it.

"She had the cheek to turn on Martie's radio," said

Tante. "But people! How sad, how solemn all music is. Perhaps that creature was not lying after all."

Even as she spoke there were small flashes of sound on the radio and the announcer spoke for some time about the shooting of the Prime Minister. Now there was no holding back the evangelist. He had propped up his bike outside the tent and stood beside it, beating the leather saddle with his fists in time to his dolorous chanting and was only to be appeased by the whole company joining in prayer.

The strangers they had picked up on the road remained with them for hours: Tante was kept busy serving coffee. Her mind was full of what she would like to do for the Prime Minister; with her own hands she wanted to nurse him, and in between making coffee and thinking what she could give all these people to eat, and cursing the Greyling for going off, she wrote out in her head a telegram: Our hearts and prayers with you in sore trial dear Prime Minister. And she decided too that she would go to church more often rather than to meetings held by the evangelist: Oubaas was the one who ran after excitement in religion. Put him in a decent, quiet congregation and he fought with ministers and elders in no time. If only they could have lived quietly on the farm away from the drunks and whores of the diggings . . .

They did not see the Greyling until six o'clock in the evening: she was running around like a mad thing, and her only wish, said Tant Bertha to me when she recounted the story, was to make herself important by telling those who had not heard that the Prime Minister was at death's door. If she had not been afraid of the dark she would have run on and on, screeching

out the dire news, a bird of ill-omen if ever there was
one, a hammerhead prophesying death to the land. But
the diggings was no place for a young Coloured girl
alone at night and as soon as the sun set she hastened
back.

On her return Tante meant to shake her and call
her a good-for-nothing but she was so relieved to see
her that she only gave her a little push. She took some
of the strain off Tante: the Greyling, whatever her
faults, was a smart little worker and she knew every
inch of Tante's ways. She soon had the place tidy and
was despatched to a hummock of ground to watch for
Maarten's coming: Tante felt nervous with him away
at Jakkalspan at a time like this. She was making a big
batch of fat-cakes and in her floury apron stood under
the stars and called to the Greyling: "Is he coming yet,
Bokkie?" to which Bokkie shrieked a reply: "Nonna,
there are two people on the road and I think one of
them is him." "Look after the fat-cakes," said Tante
and she herself watched from the hummock: the men
Bokkie had seen were hidden now by a mound of earth
thrown up out of a hole.

The faultless day had only been a forerunner of this
evening. Who could doubt the Creation, thought
Tante, standing up there as the air grew cooler and
the lustre of the stars deepened. One heard such talk
on the diggings, from people supposed to be educated,
about men being descended from apes, yet there was
Genesis for them to read: so had the sky looked at the
beginning when the first man was made by God's own
hand. But, What is to be? she asked, and it was not the
Prime Minister's fate she questioned or her own. The
question she asked was about something vast and form-

less, a cloudlike doubt that floated in her consciousness sometimes and spoiled her faith when she thought it most secure. It came of associating with the rabble on the diggings, people to whom God and Christ were only swearwords. She longed again for the farm and the veld in place of this torn earth where not a blade of grass grew.

The people Bokkie had seen were close now. They were two Natives who worked on the diggings. They were wearing short rubber boots that whispered as they went by and they smelt of Kaffir-beer and sweat. How on earth could the Greyling have thought that one of them was Martie? Tante felt like cuffing her. The Greyling had this habit of jeering at you: she could insult you without saying a disrespectful word.

"Get out there and wait," Tante spat at her, seizing the long-handled fork with which she had been turning the fat-cakes and making as though to prod her with it. The Greyling chose to take this as Tante's fun and rushed out yelling that the devil was after her. "She needs such a kick," Tante grumbled.

"Martie doesn't come," she said to the Oubaas.

"We must go back home to the farm tonight, love," said the Oubaas.

"Straight away?" said Tante joyfully.

"Yes, get packed."

In spite of her joy, Tante began to see difficulties. "What about the claim, Pieter?"

"We'll sell it."

Tante thought of the loss if they sold out of hand like that but she resigned herself for she knew by the expression of exaltation on the Oubaas's face that he was inspired so it was no use arguing with him. She called the Greyling and began to pack.

The news had been flashed on to the screen in the bioscope. Maarten with several other young men left the place and went to the police station for they thought that now surely they would be needed: the young men at Jakkalspan belonged to a skietkommando and had been waiting all month to be called up to help deal with the riots and murder that had been taking place in South Africa from the beginning of the year.

Twenty of them crowded into the police station. The sergeant, a huge bored man, said that they should go to Groenewald who was the officer in charge of their kommando.

"He's on holiday in Durban," said Maarten.

"Fancy that," said the sergeant, and snarling suddenly: "Get out and stop causing trouble."

"We want to help stop trouble," Maarten protested.

The sergeant's energy had deserted him. He yawned and went back to the study of a pamphlet. The boys drifted away. As Maarten was leaving, the sergeant said generously, "You'll get your turn, I promise you. Your names will be read out over the radio. In the meantime, go to your veld-kornet, he'll tell you what to do." Maarten was embarrassed; it was obvious that the sergeant regarded him as the rankest amateur. He wished Rottcher was there: Rottcher kept all the men in the Perelkop district in line. He was a real leader. Rottcher would have made the police sit up.

All the older men in the kommando advised them to disperse but Maarten held the group of boys together. They were without rank so he got himself elected as their leader and then ordered them to go home and get their guns: they were to meet on the Jakkalspan-Joh'burg road hard by the diggings.

When he came for his gun, he was standing like a cadet, Tante said, and his face had a military impassiveness yet underneath there was excitement which had brought out a gloss on him such as you see on a horse that is about to race. He was twenty-two and she saw this longing of his for prestige as part of those romantic ambitions of a few years before: he used to send in applications for a berth on the whalers going to the South although he had never been at sea except for an hour's excursion while on holiday in Durban.

"Your gun is on the lorry," Tante said.

He marched off to get it and began ordering the Greyling about.

"Basie, I can't take the stuff off again," Bokkie argued. "Help, nonna . . . Oubaas . . ."

Oubaas said: "No, Martie. Put all those things back. You don't need your gun. Don't think of more shooting."

"Everybody else will be armed," said Maarten. "I'm meeting the rest of the kommando down at the crossroads here."

"No, you're coming home with us to Diamant. Help load up the lorry."

"They elected me leader. I've got to remain with them."

Some of the boys had arrived at the meetingplace; there was a roaring of motor-bikes and once the crack of a rifle shot.

"Gids, this shooting is in the air today," exclaimed the Greyling.

Maarten looked at her sharply. "Are you pleased by any chance, Bokkie?"

"My dear time, no. I was the one to tell your parents that he was shot."

"I heard about that. You leave my transistor alone. A sjambok bites into you," said Maarten with a sinister crack of the fingers.

Bokkie, perhaps in an access of terror, leapt on to the lorry and with a prodigious heave pulled out Maarten's rifle from under a pile of cardboard boxes. "There, there, basie."

A number of guns went off. Oubaas paled.

"They're getting out of hand. I'll have to go and restore order," Maarten said, pleased with himself.

"Tell them to come with us to Diamant," said the Oubaas. "We'll start again on the church. Do you realize that it's four years since we laid one brick upon the other?"

Tante was more in touch with people than the Oubaas . . . he was deaf and often had the wrong impression about what was going on even when he wore his hearing-aid. Tante said: "We don't want all those boys at Diamant. There probably isn't one among them who knows a thing about building."

"We'll do it, hey, Martie?" said the Oubaas, turning his back on her. "Do you know, while I was standing in the road, it came to me like the still small voice: Why have you not built the church you promised Me?"

"There's no time now for building churches," Maarten exulted.

"Tell us about your church," Kotze was saying but the Oubaas only smiled vaguely, for Maarten was yelling: "Bokkie, you devil, find my box of ammunition," and there was no room for anybody else's voice.

The Greyling scrabbled in a packing-case. The box of ammunition was not to be found there. She plunged her hand into other boxes and felt around. Tante rushed out with the ammunition. The Greyling was in such a daze that she did not realize that it had been found and went on trying box after box. She stopped only when Tante shrilled, "You Greyling there, one day I'll take hold of you . . ."

The boys had tired of waiting at the crossroads and they now arrived outside the tent. There was such a stamping and whistling and shouting that conversation became impossible. Not all the boys belonged to the kommando, there were members of the Scooter Club present; they had been on a Club outing and joined the cavalcade leaving Jakkalspan. There were lone youths and those who had their girls on the pillions of their bikes. Some ducktails who had arrived in a car were grouped near Kotze. Maarten, having loaded his rifle, sent an experimental shot over their heads.

"Rock 'n roll, baby," he yelled.

One of the boys whipped out a bicycle chain. He was standing in the light, a tall dark boy with side levers that looked as though they had been blacked in by a burnt cork. He was wearing a leather jacket and on the back of it was written in red letters "Rock 'n roll baby" underneath the drawing of a girl in a yellow bikini.

As tall as he was, Bruggemann, the Delports' neighbour on the diggings, was taller. He had come over a few minutes before and now began to move in on the ducktail. Tante was appalled: they were going to be involved in one of those terrible incidents she had read about in the newspapers, of teenagers wrecking a place. . . . It did not come to that.

Bruggemann simply stood with his arms curved as though for an embrace: Maarten made a rush forward, determined not to be ousted from his leadership. The ducktail swung the chain.

"Fred!" yelled Bokkie from the top of the lorry, in recognition of the boy with the chain.

"So? I thought he was a Coloured," said Maarten.

Fred's companions divided, a few sticking by him, the others already on their way to the car. Men and boys moved over to Bruggemann; this was something more than a teenagers' clash.

"Since when have we to associate with Coloureds?" said Tante, urging the men on now.

Oubaas grabbed a sjambok from a pile of things on the ground. The Coloured boy stepped back slowly into the darkness. His friends, only three of them remaining, walked beside him, stiff-legged in their tight jeans: the others had fled in the car.

Kotze, ignoring all this, was still saying: "Tell us about that church."

There was the sound of running, blows and an agonized scream: the men came back in ones and twos. Maarten and Bruggemann were the last to return.

"That showed them," said Maarten.

At last Kotze had got the Oubaas to talk.

"It's like this: the name of my farm is Diamant. Why, people? Because it was bought out of the biggest diamond found on the Clarkson diggings. I promised God that if He let me find a big diamond I would build a church. Well, brothers, one day the diamond turned up in the sieve. I bought my farm, I started the church: that is, I cleared the land and marked out the building and laid a few courses of bricks, but in ten years, God forgive me, I've done no more than brush away ants from the joists and clean out the weeds that grow in the mortar. Now there is a fine modern church, all angles and with a tall spire, at Perelkop which is only about seven miles from Diamant. I've thought to myself, What does God want with my funny little church? And the minister has said that it would be more fitting if I made a donation to some charity. But a vow is a vow."

"Hear, hear."

"The minister only wants your money. You steer clear of him, oom."

"How much does he want?"

"He said a thousand pounds," muttered the Oubaas.

"Don't give it," a boy said, laughing.

"No. I'm going back to build the church now. Who will come and help?"

"Who's ready to build for the Lord?" cried the evangelist, taking out a notebook.

Not one of the boys came forward.

"There's God's work for your hands," exhorted the evangelist.

"Put away your guns and come with me to Diamant," said Oubaas.

"Build a house for the Lord! Hallelujah!"

"Put my name down, baas," said the Greyling. "Bokkie Sipho, to carry bricks and water."

Kotze wrote her name down. He began to rock himself backwards and forwards with the motion peculiar to his sect, groaning out hallelujahs. Oubaas joined him and so did Bruggemann who was one of his converts. Some of the youths cat-called but he was oblivious to them: he worked himself into a frenzy of tears and gasped out: "Lord God of hosts!" before he subsided.

Bruggemann said huskily: "Write my name down, brother," and two boys came close to him and gave their names.

Tante went on quietly loading the lorry, passing through the group with whispered apologies. She carried light bundles while behind her came Bokkie with the heavier stuff. Even now Bokkie had not recovered herself. "Dear Christ help us," she would say and stand stockstill, contemplating an invisible scene until Tant Bertha got her going again with a well-placed elbow.

"Come to Diamant," yelled the Oubaas.

"Oom, we're not going to Diamant," said one of the young men. "We're ready to help the Government, we're ready to thunder up the ones who shot the Prime Minister . . . we'll shoot all the filth plotting against us . . . we'll clean the Communists out of the country."

"You clean the country, yes," said the Oubaas. "But you must do it legally. You must wait until you are called up."

"Start to pray," called the evangelist.

"Yes, pray," said the Oubaas.

"We'll do that," said the young man, winking at Martie: he was like a person humouring a drunk.

Tante, returning from a trip to the lorry, noticed their attitude to the Oubaas. She stood there rigid, prepared to defend him but not knowing how to do it, feeling her body thick and unwieldy in its dusty black dress, and seeing these young people strong yet

19

unsubstantial in the wedge of light pouring through the tent opening.

Maarten had smiled at his mates behind his father's back. It was a wound in her heart. He would do anything to retain his hold over them but Tante knew he had already lost them for the derision they felt for the Oubaas spilled over on to his son.

Oubaas was uncomfortable suddenly. Some of the boys who had been drinking brandy were openly sneering at him.

He said to Maarten, "Get ready to leave. We're going in five minutes' time."

Tante saw that there would be a quarrel; Maarten had been drinking too.

She said, "Let Martie stay on a while. He will be needed here."

"God needs him," said the evangelist.

Tante was thinking of the claim that would be left abandoned; Bruggemann had gone off to make arrangements about his claim but so far the Oubaas had made no provision at all for settling their affairs at Jakkalspan.

"There is the labour to be paid off and the claim must be sold. And what about the picks and shovels and the machinery? We'll never get them all on the lorry. Let Martie stay behind and arrange everything."

The Oubaas felt that she had criticized him. "What is more important, the soul or picks and shovels?"

"It is only that the things will rust or get stolen and the boys . . . you can be fined for not paying them off . . ." but the Oubaas had stalked inside, pretending that it was she who had humiliated him in front of the young men. She would not defend herself: she did not mind what happened between her and the Oubaas provided that there was peace between him and Martie.

Oubaas pulled the hearing aid from his ear as a sign that he was to be left alone.

Kotze said: "Sister, you must not stand in the light of our brother."

The young people began to drift away. In the sudden silence a deep groan was heard. It must have come from one of the Coloured youths who had been beaten up.

Tante said to Bokkie: "Are you too frightened to go out there and take him a cup of water?"

"I'm frightened, nonna, but I'll go."

"No, you don't," said Maarten. "He only got what he asked for, a kick on the backside."

"Nonna?" said Bokkie with the cup of water.

"Take it to him if you want to, Bokkie," said Tante vigorously. "What's come over you, Martie? Must you be vindictive?"

Bokkie sidled past Maarten with the cup. She came back with it still full.

"I could find nobody," she said mournfully. "He must have crept away when he heard me coming." She looked with sudden boldness at Maarten. "I wish I had not spoken to Fred. People wouldn't have known him for a Coloured then."

"Is he your boy-friend?" Maarten jeered. "How do you know him?"

"He works at the tearoom," said Bokkie.

"Hullo, Fred," said Maarten. "Hullo, Mrs. Freddie."

"Now leave me alone, basie."

Tante had written out a list of the things Maarten

should attend to. He rolled the piece of paper into a tight pellet and flicked it hard at the Greyling as she staggered past with two suitcases.

"Fatherland, have you ever seen anything like it?" said Tante to the skies. "The creature will have a nervous breakdown if you tease her so."

Maarten followed Tante, speaking earnestly. "Mother, be sure to let me know what Rottcher thinks of the shooting of the Prime Minister. And when you're talking to him, let him know how I took over here. Initiative in a crisis, that's what he likes to see."

"I'll tell him, Martie," said Tante but only to pacify him: she avoided Rottcher if she could.

He was Maarten's hero, the organizer of the Perelkop Veld Guard which Tante thought of as that hotbed of politics: from it the boys sallied out to break up political meetings or protest marches, wielding two-foot planks that they kept in their lockers with their sports gear. Through this society Rottcher ruled our district though he had no legal authority. My father's Progressive friends, deceived by the huge frame, the booming voice, the naïve manner, accused him of belonging to the nineteenth century; but Rottcher was a twentieth-century man, of the fascist type.

At such a time, with violence in the very air we breathed, Tante felt she would rather have Maarten exposed to the temptations of the diggings than to Rottcher's creed, but for all that her heart misgave her as she climbed on to the lorry and left him standing by himself: she could hear the roaring of the drunken diggers on their way home from the Saturday night's carousal. She had to climb down and give him a last warning.

"Don't take up with bad women."

"No, mother."

"No drinking."

"Just a sip, mother."

"Don't gamble."

Was she mad leaving him alone here? How was her son to withstand the harlots, the cards, the brandy?

"Say your prayers every night, son. God will look after you."

"Yes, mother," said Maarten, suddenly tender. He kissed her and helped her back on to the lorry. She was comforted, he was a good boy.

Bruggemann and his wife Cissie had no possessions except a pig to worry them. Bruggemann had been working in with a syndicate of diggers and had simply handed over his share in return for twenty pounds. The only thing he could not dispose of was the pig which had an evil reputation. This was placed in a forty-four gallon drum on the back of the lorry and the Greyling screamed whenever it struggled to get out because she was convinced that it would attack her: she believed that it had eaten a Native baby who had disappeared from the diggings.

Petrus Kotze rode behind the lorry on his motorbike. He kept looking back for the boys who had promised to help with the building of the church; they never did come to Diamant. At every stop he mourned with Oubaas over the modern youth. How glorious it would have been if all the young men of Jakkalspan had accompanied them on their bikes. . . . But Tante did not mind; she would have had to feed the boys. Bruggemann alone, from what she knew of his appetite, would keep her busy at the stove all day.

CHAPTER 2

I did not know that the Delports had returned to Diamant until I saw her shopping in Perelkop. Tante and I were not great friends at that time; she was shy of me. There is a sort of arrogance you encounter in some rural women: they have had it all their own way ruling their households, they have the daily sycophancy of their servants and if they are tempered at all it is by the harshness of climate or the uncertainties of markets. I mistook Tante's shyness for this arrogance. She was a big, fair woman with a straight back and her very bearing misled me: I thought that in her heart she despised me because of my husband's crime.

There was trouble in the location that day. The Natives had stayed away from work . . . there are two factories on the outskirts of the town. At one o'clock the mobs were in the streets yelling for the release of their leaders. I wanted to fetch my son from school but I could not get through to him for a long time so I parked my car against the kerb. Natives surged all round me. For months we had lived on the edge of violence: we had known that there were agitators among our Natives. It was to be expected that after the shooting of the Prime Minister there would be trouble yet it seemed unreal to find the hordes erupting into Perelkop's quiet street. Some women were dancing naked in front of a marching column: I took these for prostitutes but my father told me afterwards that this is a primitive custom women adopt to shame their men into battle. Up and down the street the agitators raged, harrying the people with deep growls of "Afrika!" and the women were crying out shrilly like birds.

The Saracens of the police cruised slowly behind the column as though pushing it onward.

The sense of outrage that I had felt at first in seeing the Natives there without fear of the police and guns, gave way to panic; they seemed then not to be people but vast ants that had no conception of the power ranged against them. They would come on as ants do, to be annihilated by the million before they would turn aside from a chosen path. At the end of the street I heard a burst of machine-gun fire; it did not deter the mob except for one man I saw fleeing into a lane.

On the other side of the street I saw Tant Bertha swinging a shopping bag in an attempt to batter her way through the crowd flowing round her. She was frightened. A Native woman as big as herself suddenly cleared a space and danced up to her. The woman was wearing a shapeless faded pink dress and she lifted her skirt up so that I, from the back, saw her great buttocks rolling. Tante stood there staring at the woman's nakedness. Then the Greyling shot through from the pavement, head first on to the woman's belly. Four Native policemen charged and the woman was felled.

Tante and the Greyling were escorted into a shop.

At last I got my son Raymond from school and drove homewards. The road runs through a pine plantation on Diamant. It was only half a mile from there up to the house and I turned in to commiserate with Tante over her experience. The Greyling was washing her feet for her in a white enamel basin.

She sat silent, dismayed at having been caught like this, but the Oubaas spoke for her.

"She will lie down for the afternoon, hey my old treasure? She's still frightened after what happened this morning."

"I came to see if there was anything I could do to help."

Tante shook her head.

"The police are expecting trouble again tonight," said the Oubaas. "What are you going to do, Mrs. Van Doorn? You and Raymond mustn't stay alone."

"Will you go to the Rottchers?" Tante managed to say. She was holding out her foot for the Greyling to dry, and murmured: "Don't forget, in between the toes, Greyie, and then a sprinkle of powder."

"Mrs. Rottcher is in hospital in Pretoria."

"Nothing serious, I hope."

"A slight operation."

"Then you must come here," she said.

"There's not enough room, Tante."

"You and Raymond can have our room. Pieter and I are used to roughing it on the diggings."

I refused but in the end I had to accept Tante's invitation. The police sergeant rang me up to tell me not to remain alone that night. Though a cordon had been placed round Perelkop location, there was the danger of a break through. There were also agitators in the Storm valley who were trying to incite the kraal-dwellers to rise; he estimated that there were ten thousand guns in the valley.

"There, I knew you would come," said Tante, hurrying to the car to bring us in. "Your room is all ready for you."

She took us into the big front room where there was a double bed. She had good linen and she had turned back the blankets to show the hemstitched sheets. The room was heavy with crochet work which I supposed she had done during those years on the diggings; and all about were clay models that she had made.

She went round briskly, opening drawers and the wardrobe to show us where to put our things.

"I've left Pieter's suit in the wardrobe and my good dresses and suede shoes."

"It doesn't matter, we are here only for the night."

"You don't know how long this will go on. We're in laager. We must make the best of it. God knows what may happen. If they burst out of that location, we'll be wiped out. Somehow I'm not afraid of those in the valley, in spite of what the sergeant said. It's this educated Kaffir-stuff that is the danger. I've made a plan. As soon as we hear them coming, you must run and hide in the patch of weeds at the bottom of the lands. This plan is for the night time. Pieter and I will make the beds quickly, all except this one, then they'll think only Pieter and I are in the house. I've told the others to run for it too, no use all of us being killed and Pieter and I have lived our lives. You mustn't come out until I call, hear. Hear, Raymond. Natives are very cunning and you don't know who is on your side and

27

who isn't. Understand, Raymond? If I don't call, stay where you are until it gets light. By then the police will probably have reinforcements."

"And if they come in the daytime?" said Raymond.

"Then you must hide under the bed and we will have to shoot it out to the end."

The Oubaas was working under difficulties. He had no labourers because all his Natives except old Sipho, Bokkie's grandfather, and some women, had been lured away by the promise of a statement from the police and they were trapped in Perelkop location with the mob. At our farm only my overseer remained, a Coloured man Luke, and a working party of ten convicts whom he had locked in their quarters. When the Oubaas heard about these, he insisted on borrowing them so that the work on the church could go ahead more quickly. To please Tante, he mounted guard over them with a shotgun.

Petrus Kotze downed tools. No blood was to be shed on the site of the church. He and Oubaas quarrelled. Oubaas pointed out that it was his church, not Kotze's. Kotze went into the veld to meditate. Bruggemann had disappeared from the scene after morning coffee and was lying on the river bank with his head in his wife's lap. So Sipho, who had worked on the buildings in Johannesburg, had to lay bricks while the Oubaas held the shotgun. At noon Sipho went off to have some food.

The convicts packed on to the Oubaas, knocked him down and vanished with the shotgun into the Storm valley. Bokkie found the Oubaas lying there stunned when she went to call him for the midday meal.

We heard her shriek. I pushed Raymond under the bed. Tante flew round shutting the windows and doors.

"The rifle, boiling water, pepper . . . O help us, Father . . ."

The Greyling came up the pathway squealing on a sustained note. Bruggemann slept through it and had to be shaken into consciousness so that he could help carry the Oubaas to the house.

We had found Bruggemann on the river bank lying in his wife's arms.

"On the river bank," Tante whispered to me. "One can't help wondering. . . . What on earth could make Bruggemann sleep in the morning if it wasn't that he covered her like a turkey-cock out there in the open. I hope you're not shocked."

"Me? Never."

"Nor I. But you have to be careful with people when it comes to sex, especially here in Perelkop. On the diggings of course you can say what you like. But to me there is something beautiful in young married lovers."

"When I was a girl, Tante, I knew an old man who was supposed to be simple. He said to me one day: The garden of Eden is still here on earth but only lovers enter it, and very young children; everybody else is ashamed of their bodies."

"And the Lord God planted a garden eastward in Eden. . . . How often I've read it and not seen its meaning. Who was he who told you that?"

"Old Adraanse."

Tears sprang into Tante's eyes. "I'm sorry, I didn't mean to hurt you," she said: my husband murdered Adraanse's daughter.

"From the beginning I did not avoid that name, Tante, and it's ten years now."

"You must have this," she said distractedly, snatch-

29

ing the clay head of a Bushman from the mantelpiece. "And this one and this . . ." a giraffe and a lion . . . "And there's that span of oxen in your bedroom, you must have that."

"Tante, it's true, I don't mind talking about Adraanse."

But she was not convinced and at table saw that I got all the tit-bits.

She now had the Oubaas where she had wanted him from the start of the troubles, inside the house with the doors and windows locked; Bruggemann at the front window and the evangelist at the back door armed and ready. But this did not last long. The Natives had not hurt Oubaas beyond a bruise on the shoulder and the next day he was working on the church again. The evangelist was helping now that there was no danger of bloodshed on the church site and the work went forward steadily throughout the morning: in the afternoon the evangelist ricked his back and Oubaas for the rest of the time that the man was at Diamant had to rub him three times a day with liniment.

Bruggemann had gone down into the valley to try to round up the convicts; the sergeant could spare nobody to go after them. He came back defeated, having got lost in thick bush. Oubaas sent a telegram to Maarten who had hunted in the valley since he was twelve. Maarten arrived the next morning, having left an old digger in charge of the claim.

He brought the convicts back that day.

"Rottcher says I should have a medal." He was swaggering.

"It's a wonder to me that the Veld Guard doesn't issue medals," I said.

"How about you giving me a kiss since I can't have a medal?" He had found me alone on the front stoep.

"What have you done with the boys?"

"Rottcher took them over. The police are busy and if you lay a charge it means endless trouble. So he has put them to work on his potato fields. That will teach them. We gave them each a hiding too." He put his hands on my shoulders. "How about that kiss?"

I moved away. I suspected that he had had no experience with women and that was why he hung round me, a married woman older than he was. You never saw Maarten Delport with a young girl.

My father said that he was a dangerous man because he was an idealist. Rottcher scored materially out of the Veld Guard; he was a solid hunk of a man. But Maarten would have starved to uphold the policy of separate racial development; his reward was the conviction that he was superior because he was White.

It was easy enough for me to turn the talk from kissing to politics.

He did not work on the church but spent his time at shooting practice or in Perelkop with a group of men patrolling the suburbs.

For days a battle raged between the police and the Natives who had entrenched themselves in a hostel at Perelkop location and while it was on I remained at Diamant. Every morning my son Raymond stood at the window looking towards the town. If the Harvard plane was up, that meant another day at Diamant. This Harvard was used as a spotter and while the mobs were on the move you could follow their route from its flight. The whine of the engine became hateful to us.

Tante had stationed Cissie Bruggemann next to the radio to listen for the names of the boys being called up, for it would soon be Maarten's turn. I helped with the cooking in the afternoon but during the morning I went to our farm to exercise the Boxers or wandered down to watch the building. Tante was always busy. If she wasn't cooking, she was engaged in warfare against the white ants.

The house on Diamant was an old one. It had been the dwelling place of a bywoner when my husband's people owned the farm. It had been built of mud bricks about sixty years before and it was crumbling under the assault of white ants.

Tante had papered the walls and this, I felt, was what held the place together. One dared not think what was going on behind the paper. As you looked at a wall, a sandy runnel would appear.

Tante did not speak to us outsiders about the white ants. We would see her sprinkling a mysterous white powder on bread and jam; Sipho scuttled under the house or climbed on to the roof to deposit the baits. Her search was for the queen ant. One day I saw Sipho approach her with something in his closed fist. It must have been a queen ant for Tante examined it with a fat, secretive smile. That day she made the only reference to the scourge of her life.

She said, "Did you know, Raymond my boy, that the queen ant is the brain of the swarm and if she dies the whole lot die?"

There was more than one swarm in the house. The next day Tante was sprinkling white powder on bread and jam again. I heard the sounds of the ants' workings which manifested itself in the running of wood pulp or streaming of sand behind the wallpaper.

I did not sleep well at Diamant. The Delports had two rowdy dogs and their Natives kept a pack of mongrel whippets that yapped at shadows; nobody ever went out to see why the dogs barked. We kept Boxers and at the first sound of barking my overseer Luke went out to investigate. I could not get used to the hell of noise at Diamant. Tante could sleep through the symphony of the dogs but if I scraped a match to light a candle so that I could read, she would instantly pop her head through the window to enquire: "Are you feeling ill?"; at this time I think she suspected me of having designs on her son.

Once a night the Bruggemanns woke and made love. They had been married only three weeks before coming to Diamant. Oubaas recognized the state of affairs by taking it for granted that Bruggemann finished work on the church at ten o'clock each morning after the coffee-break.

Kotze did not work either, but hobbled to the site on the Oubaas's arm and read to him from a huge book written by an inspired German carpenter: Oubaas would stand sometimes for an hour with a trowel in one hand and a brick in the other while Kotze read out the descriptions of the devil in which the author specialized. Sipho, when he could be spared from the white ant hunt, laid bricks and then the Oubaas would listen in comfort to Kotze, for the Greyling was true to her promise. As soon as she thought she had finished her work for the morning, she would run down to the site and stack bricks or carry water from the spruit, an ear

33

always cocked to catch Tante's yell of rage when she discovered that she was missing.

One afternoon I went down there and found that Kotze had lulled himself and the Oubaas to sleep. The book lay open at an illustration of one of the carpenter's visions; a green and red devil with the horns of an Afrikander ox.

Sipho was laying the bricks. He was more expert than the Oubaas. Twenty-two years he had put in on the buildings, first as a concrete-pourer and then as a scaffold boy: his face was marked with deep, tragic lines from the hard work.

The Greyling was carrying bricks, with an occasional glance of terror at the devil's picture. She was a narrow little thing, about nineteen years old, lost in an old wrapper of Tante's: it came to her heels and was so wide that it swelled out like a balloon when the wind caught it.

Refreshed, the evangelist and Oubaas woke up as the air grew chilly. They were in fine form for grace before the evening meal. Oubaas, as the head of the house, led off, folding Tante's hands between his palms. Then it was Kotze's turn: he introduced two chapters from the Book of Job into the grace. I caught Tante peeping in dismay at the soup as it cooled on the table.

After the meal Oubaas said grace again and so did Kotze. We sat down at six and were not done before half-past eight. We all had a little ginger brandy then except Raymond who had Coca-Cola. Tante handed Bruggemann a strengthening egg-flip as well.

"Tant Bertha." He raised the glass. Cissie gave a tight proud smile.

Raymond would not look at them. They were al-

34

ways joined to each other, usually by interlaced fingers, sometimes by his hand to her breast where it swelled under the armpit and now while they drank awkwardly, by arms linked at the elbows. Raymond was ten years old and offended by any talk of girls and love; but the sight of their love caused a deep ache in my bowels.

Tante seemed to guess. She made the Oubaas pour out more brandy for me; and kept a sharp eye on her son.

Maarten was there that evening. He had come in late and said to me from across the table: "You may go home tomorrow if you like, Mrs. Van Doorn darling. Perelkop is as silent as the grave tonight. There will be no more trouble for a while."

Now he was sitting in an armchair looking through his collection of long-playing records, shut up into himself as though he were alone. He had a well-boned face, French like the Oubaas's, with long muscles from the cheek to the jaw: his mouth was so tender that you would never have thought him capable of brutality; yet I had seen him sjambok a Native and even now his knuckles were scarred from some fight.

He did not touch the brandy Oubaas had poured out for him. When he drank it was with a purpose, to nerve himself to an effort: he was often drunk at the Veld Guard meetings. Tante drained his glass after one or two sips; she had collected the empty glasses to take them to the kitchen for washing.

Maarten leaned back on the chair listening now to the Oubaas and the evangelist talking. Mystical stuff it was . . . God meant people to be different . . . Who was it but God who ordained the Tower of Babel? . . . there was authority for Apartheid in the Bible . . . it was a sin for White and Black to marry . . . the White man's task was not to bring riches to the Kaffir, he must bring the Kaffir to Jesus . . . that was the real community of Man, all souls were equal . . . but God meant people to be different . . . there was authority for Apartheid in the Bible . . .

"I do believe that God meant people to be different," said Tante and this was when she sipped Maarten's brandy. "After all a rose does not cross with a daisy, a cabbage does not cross with a radish. But they grow in the same bed together," she added wonderingly. "You know, I've never thought of that. Plants grow in beds next to each other or in the veld and they don't mingle. Why do we, brother Petrus?"

"God put the flowers there as an example of what He intended for us," said the evangelist promptly.

"There's no getting away from it, Petrus can answer your questions," said Tante as we went into the kitchen to wash the glasses. "He's a clever man but he needs the authority of a church and a nice house and family, instead of that he rides around like a vagabond with a kitbag on his back."

Raymond dawdled on the back stoep. Outside in the intense darkness was the little house. White ants had loosened it from its slight foundations and the wind used to knock it over. Raymond had to screw up his courage to go down there. He would not know from which side to enter because Sipho when he propped the house up put the door back anyhow. The white ants had eaten at the seat: it was obvious that somebody would fall in one day. A big stick was placed against the wall. The Oubaas notched it when a snake was killed there. I had never dared to count the notches but at a glance you could see that there were more than ten. We had been asked not to kill the file snake that was seen about sometimes: he was harmless and had been a pet of Martie's once.

Then there was the Bruggemann's pig to contend with. It was half-grown, a ferocious black thing that no stye could hold: Bruggemann boasted that it could jump six feet. A Native baby had vanished on the diggings and the mother swore the pig had eaten it. This the Delports and the Bruggemanns refused to believe for the mother was a prostitute and had probably got rid of the child herself; but Raymond, like the Greyling, believed it.

Raymond walked down the path. I hoped for his sake that the pig was well away in the orchard; it had the habit of nosing open the door of the little house, and sprawling half in and half out. Try to make it budge . . . it lay motionless even if you kicked it, evil-eyed so that you were afraid that it would snap at your leg as you stepped over.

Raymond made the excursions down there a test of his courage, he would not allow me to go down with him and wait, though he would come with me, whistling to encourage me. But tonight after pushing open the door he turned and ran away, dropping his torch.

"Whatever is it?" cried Tante and I, catching hold of him as he howled on the pathway.

"Something is in there."

Oubaas and Maarten had come out. The evangelist stood at the doorway and even the Bruggemanns had been tempted from the sofa.

"There's a ghost down there," said Tante.

"Not in a place like that," reproved the evangelist.

Oubaas and Maarten went down and caught the Greyling in there.

"Filth," we yelled at her with one voice.

Tante made her scrub the seat with Lysol. Afterwards we heard Sipho giving her a hiding . . . duuf, duuf! . . . to the accompaniment of her shrieks. Normally Tante would have sent the Oubaas to stop him but that night she said: "Good, let him thrash her. What next will she dare to do? We might get a disease. And you can be sure she is screaming louder than she need to get on the right side of me again."

Cissie then told us that she had once caught a Native girl on the diggings washing her husband's shirt and socks in the same bath as the White people's washing. It made her sick for days, just the sight of it. But the Oubaas knew one better than that. In a boarding-house where he had stayed, the houseboy had used somebody's toothbrush . . .

Raymond got ready for bed looking solemn because the Greyling was being beaten; and hid his toothbrush. Maarten had turned on his radio.

The Greyling's screams tapered into silence. From the radio came an announcement that the Prime Minister might be considered out of danger and that no reports of violence had come from any centre in South Africa. The Bruggemanns released each other but only while they joined in the evening prayers which tonight were prayers of thanksgiving. Oubaas and Kotze took turn and turn about until we nearly dropped. Maarten came in but he stood withdrawn into himself or smiling faintly at Kotze's rocking and tears.

Oubaas and Tante slept on the front stoep on iron

bedsteads placed as close to each other as possible. Maarten was at the other end of the stoep. I could hear them talking to each other.

"See, there is Orion's belt," said the Oubaas. "How puny we are. . . . My old father used to say no man should study the stars or he would go mad, dazzled by their splendour. What would he have said about these Americans and Russians trying to get to the moon and Venus? On starry nights he used to take my hand and we would go outside on to the veld. He would say, If only we had a string orchestra playing . . . he never lived to see the radio. Ag, I often think of him when I see Martie with his transistor set."

There were footsteps on the concrete path at the side of the house. They stopped at the edge of the house wall.

"It's Sipho, baas. Bokkie asks if she is sacked or must she come to light the fire tomorrow?" There was a shattering sob from Bokkie.

"Let her come," said Tante. Then, "Heaven, ag sis tog, I'll get some vaseline for the bruises." She went inside but Sipho and Bokkie had gone when she came out again.

"He said the girl would learn more quickly if she felt what he had done to her."

"They're hard, Kaffirs," said Tante.

"Yet he was right," said the Oubaas. "Of what use is it to be soft with her after such a bad fault? Let Sipho do it his own way, he knows how to handle her."

Tant Bertha settled herself in bed, sighing.

"Hypocrites," said Maarten suddenly.

"What?" cried the Oubaas.

"I said you were hypocrites. You talk about Apartheid but you don't begin to understand. The Greyling should never have been allowed to live with the Natives. She is separate from them, she's a Coloured. Why didn't you see that she was sent to live with Coloureds? She doesn't belong to the Natives any more than she belongs to the Europeans. Apartheid . . . you don't understand what it means. Bokkie would have been happy among her own people but you let her stay here and be tormented by these Blacks. Naturally they hate her. They don't want her any more than we do. Her right place is with the Coloured people."

"Tell Sipho that," said the Oubaas derisively. "Sipho never got lobolo for Bokkie's mother and so by law Bokkie belongs to him until she frees herself by paying him lobolo. Sixty-six pounds it is. So talk sense. The law allows a person to stay in any group that they are accepted in and Bokkie is accepted as a Native."

"She is not a Native and she is not treated as a Native by her grandmother or her cousins. She was treated as a Coloured and knocked about from the beginning. If you are such Christians and believe in Apartheid, why didn't you pay the sixty-six pounds to free her and let her go to a Coloured family?"

"I took her into my house, didn't I? I sent her to school," said Tante.

"You only wanted somebody to wash your feet."

"Apologize," snarled the Oubaas.

"Very well. I apologize."

"Then goodnight."

"Goodnight, son," said Tante.

"Goodnight."

"Mother," added the Oubaas.

"Goodnight, Mother," said Maarten.

When everything was quiet I heard him leave his bed. Tante slept through the barking of the dogs. Maarten hushed them. He must have been standing at the fence near the house for I heard him calling Bokkie but so softly that she could not have heard him. I remembered that Tante had told me that they played together as children.

The next morning when Raymond looked out, the sky was empty: the Harvard had been withdrawn. We were able to go home.

Tante and I saw each other nearly every day after that. A deep affection had sprung up between us: she was the first friend I had made since my husband murdered Hester Adraanse.

CHAPTER 3

He murdered Hester Adraanse six months before Raymond was born. I was young when it happened, only twenty-one. The courage in me was immense, a lioness's courage. But courage is not enough, a child's love is not enough for a woman living alone. I was hewn at as though I were a rock on a windy mountain, and at times it seemed as though nothing of womanhood remained to me. I looked in the mirror and was surprised to see my cheeks soft, and my mouth still pink as a carnation; my hair was silky whereas I had thought it would stand up round my head like wire. Not even after ten years did the drought of my womb show on the surface.

Raymond and I lived on this lowveld farm: Banghoek. We owned another farm on the highveld but I never went there for it was at Mission Falls that Ray killed the woman. If it had been possible to sell the farms I should have done so and I might have gone away, perhaps to another country, and changed our name; perhaps I should never have told my son that his father was a murderer. I do not know. As it was, Bang-hoek and Mission Falls were entailed and my son was the heir. Also my husband derived some comfort from the thought that his son would live at Banghoek where he himself was brought up, it gave him rights in the living world; and he regarded it as an affirmation of my love for him when I agreed to look after the farms. I had a power of attorney to administer the whole of the Van Doorn estate. To pay for my husband's defence I sold two farms; to Rottcher and the Delports.

The name of Van Doorn was known from one end of South Africa to the other as the name of a murderer; known beyond South Africa too for the case has often been written up. Keeping the name and living in this district was not in itself so difficult: my husband was descended from a great Voortrekker who was revered here. And Mrs. Rottcher stood by me. She brought everybody who mattered into line with her. I was not persecuted except by the charity of women more for-tunate than myself.

To my son I said when he was four: "Your father is not here because he killed someone." It meant nothing to him then, it was a seed I planted to grow with him. I thought he would have less pain in that way. I thought we should be able to talk about his father naturally and that as he grew older I would tell him all that had happened so that he would understand and pity his father and me. In the meantime I spoke to him only about his father's boyhood.

The plan worked until that year, 1960. Raymond and I were two friends always at ease with each other it seems to me now, but I realize that there must have been some reserve on his part from the time he went to school. He did not tell me that the children spoke to him about the murder yet they must have done so all along for they would have heard about it from their older sisters and brothers, their parents or even the servants. I was only thankful that he did not ask questions about his father's crime though I should have read that as a danger signal.

I used to drive in twice a day to Perelkop to take Raymond to school and bring him home. A few days after we returned from the Delports', I missed him at our usual meeting place outside the school. I strolled along the main street as far as the Church: its new pale bricks shone among the ramshackle wood-and-iron buildings of Perelkop. I went across to the bakery: Raymond loved the smell of new bread. He was not on the main street nor on any of the wide dusty avenues beyond, though I had been sure of finding him playing with the boys under some eucalyptus trees.

"Have you seen Raymond?" I called out in vain to the boys: they seemed not to hear as they struggled with each other over a rugby ball.

A little girl screeched, "She's asking where Raymond Van Doorn is." They heard her.

"He ran down to Mahomedy's store," one of the boys said.

The store was in a street where only Coloureds and a few Indians lived. Mahomedy said yes, my son had been there. He looked past me and sideways, his fingers moving constantly as though he tied invisible string.

He whispered, "Some European boys chased him, ten of them against one."

"Did they hurt him? Where is he now?"

"A Coloured girl grabbed hold of him and brought

44

him into the shop. I let them stay here until the boys went away."

"Where is he now?"

"The Coloured girl took him home. It's that girl who calls herself the Greyling."

Bokkie had walked home with him, nearly eight miles. They were sitting on the lawn with the Boxer Samson lying between them. Bokkie got up when she saw me.

"Why didn't you wait in Perelkop for me, Raymond?" I asked.

"I would have had to go on to Main Street again."

"We would have had to go past those boys, nonna."

"Since when have you been frightened of the Perelkop boys?" I asked Raymond.

He would say nothing. He sat silent while I put some sticking plaster over a cut on his forehead where somebody had hit him. After that he went away and I saw him throwing a ball for the Boxer. It was a windy day. The lawns were strewn with rose petals blown from great clusters against the walls.

The Greyling had filled her apron pockets with petals. She took them out one by one and crushed them in her hands to catch their scent.

"Nonna, the children all packed on to him," she said.

I longed for her to go away but I forced myself to look at her and answer her.

"Children fight."

"They were calling his father names." She had large grey eyes, beautiful in themselves but freakish in that khaki-coloured face. "They were calling basie names too. There is a boy Adraanse at the school, he came last week. A cousin of . . . He started it all."

45

"Thank you for helping basie."

"You mustn't think he was frightened. He fought back. I helped him only when they were all on top of him there under the eucalyptus trees."

"It's a wonder the children didn't turn on you."

"They did. And they called me a dirty bastard. Excuse. But I am used to that. For the little baas it was the first time he was called names."

"Yes."

"I was called names from the very beginning by my people. My cousins used to pull my hair out by the roots. I tell you, I used to wish I was pitch-black." She looked at me to see if I would laugh. She went on, stroking her black wool upwards so that it stood in peaks on her head. "I've been called so many names that I don't care any more, that's the truth. At home and at school too. There the Coloured kids called me Kaffirkralie because I live in a kraal. One day the headmaster called me into the office. What's this, you're not listed as a Coloured, he said. But I'm not Black, I said. I see that, I'm not blind, he said, but as you're not listed a Coloured you can't come to a Coloured school. Ag mister, what can I call myself? Where can I go to school? They threw me out of the Native school first day, the kids there got busy with stones. Shall I try the White school? He was going to hit me then but I said quickly: I'm not White, I'm not Black and the Government says I'm not Coloured. My baas . . . I went on to say . . . my mother is Black, my father is White, surely that will make me something . . . a Greyling, for instance? He laughed but he still kicked me out of the school."

"Then did you never go to school?"

"If it had not been for the nonna Delport I would

have grown up without knowing a from b. The nuns at the Mission took me in and the nonna paid for my books. I came out knowing typing and embroidery and knitting besides reading and writing. I'm supposed to go to Joh'burg to work one day. I could get a good job there."

"Why don't you go?"

"It's hard to get away," she said evasively. "My nonna relies on me."

"What did you and basie talk about on the way home?"

"I told him about when I was little and the way my cousins used to chase me like those boys chased him today."

"You did your best, I suppose. But I wish you had waited in Perelkop. Stay here and I'll get you a little present."

I gave her two shillings. She walked away with the money. She had almost reached Raymond on the lawn when she turned back and held out the two shillings to me.

"I don't want it, nonna."

"You take it," I said threateningly.

"Please, missis."

"Why won't you take the money? Are you being cheeky?"

She struggled to say something. When she saw the beginning of anger in my eyes, she put the money in her pocket, nodded her head as though to appease me, and walked away quickly, avoiding my child and the dog on the grass.

In the evening when I went to tuck Raymond in I saw that he was crying.

I said, "Raymond, you must be brave. It is true that your father killed someone but there was a reason, a good reason. He did it for you and for me. He loved us."

He turned his head away without answering. I was afraid; my fortitude had its roots in him. I had one of those awe-inspiring glimpses of the solitude of my spirit that had haunted me since childhood: I had thought myself done with it in the euphoria of my intimacy with him. I wanted to hold him to me and cry out to him not to leave me. This was another birth and I shook with the pangs of it.

I went from his room without knowing why he had cried.

Raymond came back to me. During the night he crept into my bed. He was a big child but with delicate wrists and ankles that I liked to encircle with a thumb and finger. I felt his cheeks wet on my shoulder.

I whispered, "You need not go back to that school again. Stop crying now, those boys will never hurt you again."

"It isn't that," he said.

"What then?" I thought, Now must I put before him the whole subtle problem of his father's crime?

"It's Bokkie," he said.

That was a relief but there was a core of jealousy to it.

"She had fifty thrashings in one month when she was my age," said Raymond, sobbing for the Greyling. "Her grandfather had to go to Joh'burg for a month. He always looked after her and when he was gone there was nobody for her to run to. He only hit her when she was bad but the others hit her because she was Coloured. You know the stick the Delports keep in their little house. She had one like that and every time she was beaten she notched it."

"Do you believe that?"

"She was going to kill the people who hit her. Then Tant Bertha noticed her and took her into the house and afterwards sent her to school. She has forgiven everybody now."

"Would you like to go to school in Bedfordview? You could stay with Grandpa and come home at week-ends."

"You said I must never run away."

"It wouldn't be running away if you went to Perelkop school until the end of the term."

"All right."

He fell asleep. Now perversely I wanted to wake him and talk to him about his father, about Hester Adraanse and the terrible boulders at Mission Falls where she had bled to death.

I did wake him up. "You must love your father, Raymond."

"Yes," he said and slept again without remembering that we had spoken.

It proved unnecessary to send him away then. The story of the children's fight with him had got round Perelkop. Mrs. Rottcher, who came home the day after, saw to that. Some parents even punished their sons for their share in the attack, there was a spate of visitors to Banghoek and unexpected presents for Raymond. The headmaster advised me not to take him away; a few of the seniors would keep their eyes open for signs of bullying. Raymond was not popular at that school but he did make a few friends.

Mrs. Rottcher had spoken to the minister about the

incident and on the Sunday following he preached at the boys. I remember Mrs. Rottcher saying to me: "A lovely sermon. There must be nothing narrow in Christianity or it ceases to be Christianity, not so?"

We were standing outside the church just before getting into our cars; her eyes were busy, noting who had come to church. She had already pointed out the Adraanse boy to me; he bore no resemblance to those other Adraanses. Women were smiling at us, at Raymond and me especially. Mrs. Rottcher glowed. She liked to point out to the community where its Christian duty lay and she liked to see it following that path. Indeed her charity seemed all-embracing.

The Kinders passed. They had with them their youngest son who had turned out to look like a Coloured; crinkly hair, thick lips and flat nose, he had them all. But his hair was reddish and his skin freckled so he would have no difficulty in being registered as White. His parents brought him to church every Sunday in a neat dark suit and highly polished shoes. He was accepted in Perelkop, with a tug at the heartstrings. The reminder of a Hottentot wife taken by a lonely Dutch pioneer? A freak perhaps? Whatever he was, young Kinder rested in the shade of our compassion. A harsher community might have argued that God had set the curse of Ham on him for some divine purpose and that he must suffer accordingly; elsewhere I have heard such an argument in the case of a Coloured-looking child born to White parents. But the Perelkop community, led by the Rottchers, was not unnecessarily cruel. Apartheid there must be but let there be charity too. I think Mrs. Rottcher looked upon the youngest Kinder boy with the pity one feels for a deformed person. Not by a look would she betray that she noticed his features and hair, any more than she would have stared at a cleft lip. If there had been the slightest suspicion of the boy's mother having been betrayed into a moment's lust with some Coloured man, Mrs. Rottcher would have destroyed her and her son too; I am more than ever aware of that now.

I had reason to be thankful for Mrs. Rottcher's charity which embraced my husband's crime. She had been tireless for ten years defending us. I was not fond of her, she was too much of the politician for me, a little conscious of her broadmindedness; and there was something hard in her, a wall of granite behind that courteous, easy-going manner. I knew that if I were to come out with any of the opinions I had been brought up to, Mrs. Rottcher would have turned on me. But I had done with my father's teachings when I decided to marry Ray and so I got on well with her; though when thinking about her I always called her Mrs. Rottcher: to her face it was Tant Rita.

Tant Bertha in the full glory of her best black dress and with a stiff black hat on her shining hair, walked in front of us. Oubaas accompanied her but Maarten Delport was with us. Rottcher had gone to a conference in Johannesburg and Maarten had been staying at Harmonie with Mrs. Rottcher.

Mrs. Rottcher always drank coffee with me on Sunday mornings on the way home from church. Today the Delports also came. It seemed to me that she was not pleased: this was the first time I had invited them. She noticed at once that a friendship had sprung up between Tante and me and chaffed me gently about it while Maarten was escorting his parents back to their lorry.

"What do you and Tant Bertha find to talk about, Ilse? You're such a bookworm and she never opens a book."

"We talk about Maarten and the building of the church."

"What else?"

"Her childhood in Angola."

"They were very poor, I believe. And after Angola . . . ?"

"The diggings."

I did not want to reveal Tante to Mrs. Rottcher and she sensed this withholding. She was hurt. Suddenly she lashed out at me.

"The other day when I was at Diamant . . . my son has bought the trees in their plantation you know . . . I saw Raymond in the Kaffirkraal with that Coloured girl. He was eating some mealiepap. Goodbye, dear." She kissed me. "I thought I should tell you about Raymond."

"Thank you, Tant Rita."

My husband had built a beautiful house at Banghoek. Raymond had been brought up in its shining rooms yet now he forsook them to sit in a kraal.

I said to him that evening: "You must not go among the Natives. You are a little White boy. If you want to play you can remain with a friend in Perelkop after school and I will pick you up later or you can bring a friend here and I will run him home. But you must not play with the Natives or even with Bokkie. That sort of thing is all right when you are very small but not now. You should be ashamed to be seen eating in a kraal."

He listened to me. He stayed at home, he invited friends from school or went to their houses to play.

But during the July holidays he brought home a pup that was almost dead, a mangy poor little thing crawling with lice; and it was a bitch. He had found her on a rubbish heap at Diamant. Natives had thrown her there to die.

"We must take it to the S.P.C.A. tomorrow," I said. He was standing obstinately with the pup in his shirt. I flew into a rage with him. "A filthy Kaffir dog. What next?" His head drooped beneath my anger. "Give me the thing, I'll get rid of it."

"What will you do with it?"

"Drown it."

He went pale. Standing there with the mangy pup against him, he said: "He tried to drown her, didn't he?"

"You're being wicked, Raymond. To hurt me for the sake of a mongrel you picked up off the rubbish heap."

"It's true. He wanted to drown her."

"Do you know exactly what happened?"

He traced a circle on the wall with the pup's limp paw. "He wanted to drown her."

"One day when you are older you will feel sorry for him."

He turned his back, not on me but on the Boxer that was jumping up at him in jealous anxiety.

"Give me that pup, I'll take it to the S.P.C.A. tomorrow."

Without answering, he ran away. The Boxer Samson, lithe and gleaming, leaped beside him.

"Just let Samson get at it," I shouted: Samson hated Natives, it had been bred into him, he killed their dogs.

I did not see Raymond for an hour.

Then he said, "I took the pup to the S.P.C.A."

"Did you walk into Perelkop and back again, all in an hour?"

"I got a lift."

At suppertime I saw him sweep up crumbs from the table and put them in his pocket; he had hidden the pup somewhere.

There is a great rock near the house. I watched from behind it, spying on Raymond like a hungry mistress. He had hidden the pup under an oak tree in the avenue near the Native quarters. He fed her with the crumbs he had taken and gave her water. She was lying on an old sock of his under a rickety shelter of corrugated iron.

It shamed me that he should have deceived me in charity to the pup. I was afraid. He must know that his father had stamped on Hester Adraanse's face as she lay dying: did he think of her as he fed the pup?

My fear made me vicious. I wanted to destroy the pup. When he was in bed, I crept to the place, meaning to take her away and have her killed. She was not there. I thought she had crawled away and I felt about in the darkness but without finding her. She was in bed with Raymond. I found her on his pillow when I went in to look at him.

He had distrusted me too much to leave her unprotected. She was still at my mercy for he slept so soundly that he did not stir when I picked her up. She was dying of starvation. I could have left her with Raymond and he would have woken in the morning to find her dead on the pillow beside him. But I fed her with an eyedropper throughout the night and saved her life.

Raymond named her Foeitog. On cold nights he smuggled her into the house and let her sleep with him. It was part of the ritual of his going to bed for me to slap the blankets to find her. She grew cunning. She learned to lie still beneath Raymond's knees when I was feeling for her and so spent many a night with him.

In time she had the run of the house and gardens. She was a disgrace; yellow, with a narrow whippet head. Nothing fattened her. And for all the love that Raymond gave her, she was not his dog: she would follow anybody on the veld if she thought there was a chance of a hunt. She lived only while she hunted.

Maarten Delport used to pass through the farm on his way to the boundaries or the valley: Foeitog had only to see him with his gun and she would follow him. No matter what stratagem he used to evade her, she would appear miles away in the veld and tag after him. In the end he trained her to the gun.

Luke, my overseer, would have liked her for his dog. Luke was a lonely man, disfigured by a birthmark like a crimson mask on his face; but he was no hunter and though Foeitog would accept food and shelter from him, she would never follow him on his solitary walks in the veld. Nor would she have anything to do with me, or any other woman.

When she came in season, I kept Samson locked in his run, but he got at her somehow and at ten months she produced four of his progeny. I suspect that a Native boy dropped her into the run one night. At any rate, Foeitog and her pups disappeared when this boy left. She had been a nuisance and her pups were an embarrassment yet I missed her; she brought me close to Raymond.

But that July I used to wake up at night with a feeling of terror in my heart: a Kaffir dog has come between Raymond and me, I would say aloud. It sounded monstrous spoken out like that. First the Greyling, then the abandoned pup . . . I wished I need never see either of them again.

I learned that neither the Greyling nor the pup stood between us: it was an idea, perhaps a revelation, that had taken my son from me.

That year it happened that the full force of the slump in timber hit us. The shooting at Sharpeville and the state of emergency aggravated the bad times, yet we were urged to raise the wages of the Natives. Rottcher told us not to do it. Far from raising the wages, we should reduce them to meet our losses, he said. Concessions would only lead to more and more demands and the next thing we would have Kaffirs asking to sit on the Town Council.

I was accustomed to following his advice, but I told him right away that I would not reduce wages: there were too many difficulties already for a woman alone on a farm. He did not quarrel with me on this point but it was understood that I was not to take on any Native who might leave my neighbours because of lowered wages.

Rottcher and the other farmers cut wages to ten shillings a month all round. Rottcher was safe in doing this because his farm hands were in debt to him and they could not leave; except a man named Tomas. He had kept himself free of debt and as soon as the cut was announced he gave in his notice.

Rottcher knocked him down but Tomas was adamant. There was no legal way of stopping him and his family from leaving so Rottcher thought of a way to trick him. Tomas had hired a lorry in Perelkop to remove his family and furniture. When the lorry arrived at his gates, Rottcher refused the driver permission to enter and the lorry was driven back to Perelkop. Tomas was left waiting at the huts and not until sunset did he find out that the lorry had been turned back. Rottcher sent his boss-boy to lock the huts that Tomas had been living in and a guard was put on them for the night. Tomas was told to clear off the farm with his family and goods before sun-up otherwise he would be arrested for trespass.

Rottcher expected Tomas to come to him for permission to enter the huts for it was a cold night. Then he would give Tomas shelter in exchange for a contract at the new rate. If he refused and spent the night in the open on the farm Rottcher would threaten to have him arrested for trespass unless he gave in. Every door on that farm was barred against Tomas. It went without saying that Rottcher's neighbours . . . I was one . . . would have him arrested if he came on to their land. He did not expect that they would be able to reach the main road before daylight since there were two old women and a pregnant girl in the party.

Tomas held out and at midnight Rottcher went to bed with the intention of threatening him with the police in the morning. At some time during the night Tomas and his people drifted on to Banghoek, carrying their possessions. A freezing wind blew from the Berg, it was real pneumonia weather. In the morning Luke came to tell me that these people were on my land and had asked permission to light fires. I told Luke that it would be better if they did not light fires as that would put me in enmity with my neighbour but I gave him a paraffin tin full of hot tea and several loaves of bread for them. Luke said that Tomas had walked to Perelkop to get the lorry. It might be a few hours before he returned.

"I will have to charge them with trespass, Luke," I said before he could ask me to do more for them: Luke was not tough.

"Basie Raymond is down there with them," he said.

"Tell him to come home at once."

"I told him and told him. He won't come, nonna."

"I'll go down and get him now."

I had to go and face those creatures who had been in the wind all night. I meant to jerk Raymond away and give him a hiding. I did not do it. He had taken off his clothes to give to the Natives: he was naked in the bitter wind. I made him put on my jacket and asked Luke to carry him home.

Once I was there, how could I refuse permission for the lighting of fires? The creatures were all shivering. There were several babies among them, the luckiest for they had the warmth of their mother's backs. They were quiet, indeed the whole troop was quiet, yet I had the impression of wails coming from them: their faces were contorted into the grimace of tears. I expected an outburst of joy when I gave permission for fires to be lit but there was not one sound. The women stood there for a few seconds, their mouths turned down in sculptured folds, before they moved to light the fires. Yet they were grateful. A month later a young girl brought some bead mats for me and a hide shield for Raymond that had taken many hours to make. Tomas had put a hundred miles between himself and Rottcher and she travelled far to bring the gifts.

One of the babies was sick. I took him up to the house and sat by the kitchen fire with him, dosing him and rubbing camphor on his chest.

"Oom Rottcher rang up," said Raymond. "He knows Tomas's people are here. He thinks you have already sent for the police. You mustn't."

"I'll have to. I don't want to but we can't take a Native's part against Oom Rottcher, my boy."

He had dressed himself but he was still wearing my jacket: Raymond always liked to have something of mine about him and you would see him sniffing at it, delicately, to catch a trace of the perfume I used. Now he took the jacket off and laid it on a chair.

"Go and hang it in the wardrobe," I said without taking in the significance of his gesture.

He went away obediently.

The mother had crept into the kitchen, bringing in a smell of woodsmoke and dirty clothes that lingered after Tomas had fetched her away. As the baby grew warm, he fell asleep. I told his mother to stay by the fire until the lorry came.

I looked about for Raymond. He should have been here where it was warm but I did not worry because I thought he had gone back to bed.

He was not in bed but alone in the icy sitting-room. I saw him there when I came in to telephone the police.

"But what are you doing in here, shivering? You'll catch your death of cold."

He muttered something and would not look at me. I rushed over to him and seized him by the shoulder.

I was going to hit him because I knew suddenly why he had taken off my jacket. He struggled with me. My fingers clutching him left bright weals on his hands. I got him into a corner of the room but then I did not hit him. I was afraid of him again. At the heart of all my dealings with him now there was the fear that he would judge me as my father had done because I loved a brutal murderer.

"Should I have turned on him and rended him?" I said but he did not know what I was talking about.

I left him and sat down but he continued to crouch against the wall where I had driven him.

"Raymond, you are too young to say what is right and wrong. I have to run the farm, I have to keep in with the Rottchers. They made our lives possible here, they've been kind to us. White people can't go against their own for the sake of a Native."

He said, "Listen, it's a lorry. It's Tomas's lorry."

If I could have said to him: Tomas has done wrong, he will have to be punished. . . . In this damned place where Rottcher was king a Native did right as long as he worked faithfully, and wrong when he loafed or gave notice.

I said at last, "Very well, I won't lay a charge against Tomas." Then Raymond was mine again and put on my jacket and sniffed at it.

In the kitchen I took the baby from his mother and gave her something to eat. There were footsteps on the path. I nerved myself for I thought Rottcher had come to check up on Tomas's arrest.

It was Tant Bertha. She had been out picking aloes and had brought a huge bunch for me.

"I've walked miles," she said: her cheeks were bright.

"What are you doing with that little creature on your lap?"

"It's one of Tomas's grandchildren. They were all out in that wind last night."

"I know." Her voice rang out: "What's the matter, Tomas? Why do you want to kill your children? so obstinate . . ." for Tomas was at the door. He stood quiet, holding his hat against his chest.

"Rottcher would be annoyed if he saw you. He's a hard man that when he starts anything."

"The child is sick."

"I can see it."

Tomas moved beseechingly. I gave the child to his mother and they went away.

Tante and I drank coffee. "Never mind what Rottcher says, Ilse. You did the right thing helping that child. Who knows? When the Black hordes descend on us to massacre us, as it might happen in the years to come, perhaps this little Kaffir of yours will put a mark on the door and you will be passed over, like the Israelites in Egypt."

"I didn't lay a charge of trespass against Tomas."

"My time, now you're in trouble. Ilse, what possessed you?"

"Rottcher shouldn't have done that to them."

"We must stand together, you know. You don't want it to be like the Congo here. And after all, everybody else cut wages."

She was not pleased with me but I walked part of the way home with her.

"You don't want to get the reputation of being a little brother to the Kaffir," she said cautiously.

61

"I dared not have Tomas arrested. Raymond would never have forgiven me."

Instantly she brightened: she could understand a mother doing anything to please her son.

"He's tenderhearted. Then you did right. They grow hard soon enough. Sometimes when I listen to Maarten talk I'm bewildered. Whatever you do, Ilse, keep your son out of the Veld Guard. You know what they made Maarten do . . . thrash two Natives . . . These Natives were had up for taking part in the riots but the Court found them not guilty. The Veld Guard said they were guilty and decided they should be punished. It fell on Maarten to do it. My son . . . He was so strange for days afterwards. It is one thing to hit a person who has made you angry but to hit a person you have never seen . . ." She stooped and picked a tiny pale veld flower, and held it from her at arm's length. "How serene it is. Like a shining pool . . ."

Tomas's lorry was on the road. We were able to see it sharpen against the sky, then it was obliterated by the curve of a hill.

"So Tomas. You beat your baas." Tante looked at me shrewdly. "Mrs. Rottcher won't drink coffee with you next Sunday, Ilse."

CHAPTER 4

The Greyling stopped me as I was walking through the Delports' plantation on my way to visit Tant Bertha. She had been sitting on a log by the roadside, reading a page of a newspaper that she must have found blowing about; it was stained and ragged. When she saw me, she threw the paper aside and sprang to her feet. Somebody had given her a black eye.

"I ask for a job, nonna."

"From me? Why do you want to leave the nonna Delport?"

"I want to learn more fancy ways."

"Well, I can't take you."

"The nonna said I could go."

Still I shook my head. I did not want the girl near me. She was too deeply implicated in the change in my son. Besides, she was tied to Diamant through her grandfather Sipho. He was so hopelessly in debt to the Oubaas that neither he nor any of his dependants ever saw money: it was a case of book entries only. I could not see the Oubaas allowing Bokkie to go.

I walked on, with her trotting behind me. She kept saying, in a voice as plaintive as a bird's, "The nonna says I can go."

As we approached the house, she darted ahead of me and went crying to Tante.

"Really you may take her," Tante said to me when she had chased her out of the room. "Pieter talked it over with me. It was Maarten's idea originally. He always thought we weren't fair to Greyie, that she should be taken away from her Black relations. And Pieter agrees with him now. Greyie got a hiding the other day: Pieter says they'll go too far one of these days and kill her. Sipho swears none of them did it . . . well, he has always been good to Greyie and they do a lot to her behind his back."

"I don't want her."

"Why not? She's excellent and you'll be doing her a kindness."

I would tell anything to Tante at this stage.

"You remember the day Raymond walked home with her?"

"Did she try anything? Heaven, did she interfere with him?"

"Not in the way you mean, not physically. Worse really. She made him see things in a different light. She only talked to him. All the way home she told him about her sufferings as a child. From that day he changed and I've had nothing but trouble with him."

"It's true, she suffered as a child. The father was some low White man in Joh'burg who ran away before she was born. Her mother went to the bad and cleared off three days after the event. Sipho hasn't heard of her for years. Greyie's Black cousins were terrible to her, so was her grandmother. Mind you, can you blame them? Who wants a bastard? That's life. But tell me, how was Raymond changed?"

In words I found shame. "He brought a Kaffir dog into the house. And you know he gave his clothes to Rottcher's Natives and would not let me lay a charge of trespass against them. So many things . . . He tasted suffering when the boys hit him because of his father's crime and now he wants to take the suffering of the whole world on his shoulders."

She said, "We must be careful, Ilse. If we find Christ's footprints in the veld we must follow them. God may have chosen Bokkie to lead Raymond to salvation. Don't be hard on her because of it."

"He threw his father's crime in my face, Tante. He judges his father and me."

"But if you are kind to Bokkie he will see your real nature. Take her and you bind him closer."

"Very well. I'll take her."

"Perhaps she and Luke will make a match. That would suit you. Luke would be more contented with a wife. It would be difficult for Bokkie to marry into a respectable Coloured family like Luke's because of the pitch-black relations but then Luke has that birth-mark. Girls won't go near him. He'll get a bargain in the Greyling, she's so smart and well-educated too and very pretty for a Coloured.

"I'm getting old, Ilse, I want to make matches right and left, hey? I never thought I would come to it, but I even wish Maarten would marry. A girl would take his mind off politics and make him less tensed up, don't you think so? Bruggemann has got a pretty sister, so fair. She is mother's help in a big family near Jakkalspan. Maarten seemed to like her. Well, I'd want my grandchildren to be fair." She began to laugh. "A grandchild would be a good idea in this house. Do you know, Pieter . . . the other night . . . it was just as if I were a young woman . . . I don't feel ashamed exactly but I wonder if people of our age have a right in that garden of Eden you told me about. A grandchild would make Pieter realize my age." Tante laughed on, a little red in the face.

I liked to sit here in her big clean kitchen, on the edge of the peace that flowed from her. She kept herself free of politics except that she supported the Republican campaign in memory of her parents. What she wanted was to be a part of the Perelkop church community. She suspected that she, the Oubaas and Maarten might be looked down upon as vagabonds because of their life on the diggings and to show people how respectable she was at heart wore black cashmere stockings and shoes with thick low heels. Her best dresses were of heavy black marocain, one embellished with jet beads and the other with a silver brooch; her house dresses were shapeless wraps of black-and-white prints. She possessed a heap of jewellery worth thousands of pounds yet never wore anything except the broad gold band of her wedding ring. Her hair was scraped back into a tight bun and she never powdered her face. But her body though stout was firm, with layer upon layer of flesh moulded to the handsome bones: her hair was golden, her face rosy and her blue eyes like a child's in their milky whites. In spite of all her efforts she aroused the venom of the Perelkop ladies by looking closer to forty than fifty.

Her manner too betrayed the sober clothes. Even

66

her shyness was part of an incorrigible youthfulness. There was a glow to her. She would mourn because some day she must die and leave the veld. I've seen her take flowers in her hands and squeeze them in an ecstasy of love. Often she would abandon her household for a few days and turn to clay to express this ecstasy. Her hands were not plump but bony as they had been in youth, and strong from working with clay. Wonderful little spans of oxen she fashioned . . . wagons, Native heads, and beasts of the veld: they sprang out of her fingertips in dun and brown or splashed with white, their muscles unerringly placed.

It was an art she had learned as a child on a river bank in Angola where she was born. When she was eighteen, an uncle paid for her and her brother to come to South Africa; their parents had left them destitute. Her brother was nineteen and had never been to school. He was sent to a hostel near Potchefstroom. He used to light a fire in the dormitory and cook rats to eat; he was used to hunting for his meat and the rats were all the prey he could find near the school. A tall fair boy her brother was who never adjusted himself to the new life and died after six months at school.

Tant Bertha had learned to read and write so she remained on the diggings with her uncle. That dazzling fairness, preserved through centuries in Africa, brought her seven proposals before the Oubaas claimed her. He was a widower twenty years older than she was and had a family of five but he was a catch among the hard drinkers and gamblers of the diggings.

They were married six years before Maarten was born. Oubaas blamed the delay on the quinine they had to take during their wanderings to keep fever at bay; but the truth was that there was a flaw in Tante. She said that she had had the best of marriage. Her stepchildren were in Rhodesia and had never bothered her: to the Oubaas she was not only a wife but the sweetheart he had found in his middle years. He did not torture her as a younger man might have done. Their life together had been placid on the whole.

Then there was Maarten. The youth that she had missed in the Oubaas she found in her son. He was the troubled wave on the waters of her life. She lived intensely loving him and found during his years of growing up all those intricacies of emotion forfeited in her marriage.

"But were you never in love with anybody besides the Oubaas?" I asked her that day.

"Yes. Once with an Englishman."

Even in this, Tante considered that she had been lucky for by loving this one Englishman she had freed herself of hatred towards a whole nation.

She had been brought up in the iron bonds of hate. Her sisters had perished in a concentration camp, her mother had had her furniture chopped up and her house burnt to the ground . . . the tale of wrongs was recounted each day at prayers into the ear of the Almighty. This hatred that she had for the English had seemed to her a law of God, like her separateness from the Blacks and Coloureds. She was taught that she must rinse her mouth if she should ever speak a word of English, she wiped out her ears if she heard English spoken. An Englishman's body, said her mother, had a deformity too frightful to name: a Boer girl who saw a naked Englishman during the war went raving mad.

In South Africa she had to get used to hearing English but she would not learn to speak it; she wiped out her ears with a disinfected cloth every night before she said her prayers; she believed that her brother died because the teachers tried to force him to learn English.

The Englishman she fell in love with had a claim adjoining the Oubaas's at Warrenton. She spat when he passed her. That redneck, she called him.

He got a fever. One afternoon his boy came running to Tante to ask for help. The Oubaas was away at the store in the township and did not get home until evening. Tante told the boy to go to the hell, him and his baas. All afternoon she busied herself with a head she was modelling. It was a hot afternoon. When she went out for a breath of air, she saw the Englishman crawling across the broken ground towards the shade of a dusty little tree that had more thorns than leaves.

Tante picked up the wasted form from the hot earth and carried him to her tent. She bathed his body with cool water and vinegar to bring the temperature down. He was so dirty that she had to take off all his clothes, praying as she did it for she remembered her mother's story of the mad girl. He was perfect, a small man and as supple as a child.

All this happened before Maarten was born and she loved the Englishman with a tenderness that she had never given the Oubaas, a prelude to what she would feel for Maarten one day.

They never kissed. The Oubaas saw to that. He was so suspicious that he had his niece to stay with them, a thin witch of a girl who never seemed to need rest and who could crochet all day without ever looking at the pattern; she it was who had made all the lace I had taken for Tante's work. So Tante only knew her love's body from having bathed it that first afternoon when she brought him into her tent.

He went away as soon as he was well and she never saw him again. The niece was on the next train to her home in Barberton.

Oubaas for a while became a fierce lover, he bound Tante fast to him. And she was like a goddess. It seemed to her in those days that she was moving as majestically as a great cloud driven by the wind. Her mind that had been pinched by hatred opened wide, and not only her mind, her womb too: her son was conceived.

There are bushveld farms that are only a stretch of grass and trees beneath the sky: you always have the feeling that they are waiting for you to move on as others did before you. All sorts of people have been here: a million warring Natives, Voortrekkers, hunters, missionaries, English soldiers, prospectors, miners, storekeepers. The land was wide, people only tasted of it and trekked on. Not so Paulus Raymond Van Doorn, my husband's greatgrandfather. He outspanned here in 1840 and died here twenty years later. In the cemetery at the foot of the hill there is a monument to him, an obelisk visible for miles around. He is a hero in this district: he fought the Zulus at Blood River and he was a great hunter. When he was magistrate, he bought vast tracts of land from the chiefs and they say he and his descendants were cursed by an old Native woman whose village he burnt down when taking up Banghoek. The Van Doorns believe in the curse and in every generation, it seems to me, do something to bring disaster on themselves: old Paulus Raymond himself, hunting alone at night as though seeking death, was trampled by an elephant. He was paralysed for six years before he died. He considered this as part of the price he paid for Banghoek and that was why he entailed it. "Destroy the heathen and let Van Doorns drink for evermore from the fountain in the hollow as I did": he had these words written into his will which is preserved in the museum at Perelkop.

Two rooms and a stoep remain of the first house he built. I stored mealies there.

I could not put the Greyling in with the Native women so I had Luke nail some asbestos and lattice round the stoep of the old house to make a room for her. Mrs. Rottcher found me there on the day I went down to inspect Luke's work.

We sat together in the shade of the rock and looked at the house and across the bushveld which stretched beneath us, a level tract running into hills and krantzes.

Mrs. Rottcher had not forgiven me for siding with Tomas but she had not quarrelled openly with me: she regarded me as a Van Doorn. Her cult was Voortrekker-worship and to her the name stood not for the name of a murderer but for the image of Paulus Raymond. Also she had a kink: she generally looked for the oblique cause of a person's behaviour as a Native looks for witchcraft when cattle die. Her mind had fastened on Tant Bertha as the cause of my shortcoming: this was the only new influence in my life and she disliked the Delports except for Maarten.

"That house of Paulus Raymond Van Doorn should be a national monument," she declared. "I'll bring the

71

Committee out one day, you'll see. It is a shame to put a Coloured in there."

"Well, it was inhabited by rats and snakes. Luke had a regular massacre. And I don't suppose Bokkie will be there for long."

"Oh?"

"I think she is after Luke."

"Why is Bertha parting with her?" I had the feeling that her whole visit was directed to this remark. Her face when I glanced at it seemed ancient and lit from within by a mocking intelligence.

"Tant Bertha is the kindest soul in the world. She is thinking only of Bokkie's good, she wants to lift her into the Coloured group where she belongs."

Mrs. Rottcher smiled and nudged me gently with her elbow, then pulled the lower lid of her eye down: "See any green in it, Ilse?" From her the gesture was coarse for her manners were usually grave. "Bertha was saying only a few weeks ago that she would always have somebody to wash her feet when she was old, meaning this Greyling of course. You must admit it is astonishing that she has let her go."

"Bokkie was taught at the Mission to do embroidery and typing," I explained with a sudden premonition of danger. "Tant Bertha feels that she should advance herself."

"Praiseworthy," said Mrs. Rottcher, getting up and shaking the grass from her skirt. She laughed. "Embroidery and typing. Are you going to let her do embroidery and typing, Ilse?" She had a way of putting you in the wrong: I found myself blushing. "There is something up, Ilse. Has the girl been making eyes . . ."

"Mrs. Rottcher!"

"Mrs. Rottcher," she jeered. "Not Tant Rita any more? Has the girl been making eyes at the Oubaas?"

"It's in the cause of Apartheid," I spat at her.

"There, I was only teasing." She gave me a charming smile but I was still a little frightened of her; and she had sown a seed of doubt in my mind. Bokkie spent hours alone with the Oubaas helping him build his church. Even the fact that Tante had told me that the Oubaas had made love to her recently assumed significance. She might have said it to throw me off the track.

Bokkie with her newness sent up an eddy of laughter at Banghoek. I began to like her. I needed talkative people about me. There was silence enough in that grave on the highveld, silence enough for my husband too. Soon I dismissed the doubt I had had about her and the Oubaas: she was not insolent, she did not flaunt herself as a Coloured girl would do who had been carrying on with her master.

And she made Luke happy. I used to hear him playing his gramophone to her in the evenings, or strumming on his guitar. I sat at my window until late. Night after night there was nothing to be heard on the farm except that once or twice I heard a subdued murmuring, of lovers courting; from Bokkie's room behind the rock. I felt contempt for myself because I listened. I thought, Are you so starved that you must follow the Coloured girl's affair? . . . are these the crumbs you snatch at? . . . It was no use. There was balm in those soft voices.

"Bokkie and I are going to be married," Luke said to me at the end of the month when he came for his wages.

"I wish you happiness, Luke."

"Thank you, nonna. I ask for a few weeks off to go and see my mother. It's awkward. There is the question of lobolo. My mother has saved a hundred pounds for me out of the money I send her every month. She won't like me paying lobolo like a Native but Bokkie says Sipho will take us to Court if I don't pay. There are difficulties. She is listed as a Zulu and my mother is not going to like that."

Luke had been with me for six years: he was a wonderful hand with the labour but he had had no success with women. He was a big man yet he had the name of being a coward in a fight; and I once saw him get sick when I was stitching up a heifer's side where the bull had gored her. I was glad that he had found somebody at last.

A cousin of his, Japie, came to take his place while he was away. I needed somebody responsible on the farm to keep guard over the convicts: they were not dangerous men but short-term prisoners who had been sentenced for offences against the pass laws or had been caught drinking illicit liquor. As a rule they worked well, anxious to get back to their jobs, but they had to be locked in the shed at night and kept under surveillance during the daytime. I had tried White managers but they took all control from me or drank or came courting me; a Coloured overseer suited me.

Luke had been gone for a few days when at midnight I heard somebody speaking to Bokkie in her room.

"Was Japie in your room last night?" I asked her when she came in to do her work the next morning.

"Yes, nonna," she said and I felt suspicious of such

a ready admission. She was dusting the furniture and she bent her head until it was almost touching the arm of a chair. I saw that her body was rigid and that she went on polishing in one spot.

"I don't want you causing trouble between Japie and Luke. Go and fetch him here, I'll give him a talking to."

"It wasn't Japie."

She had begun to sweat. Suddenly she looked up at me and I saw that her mouth was twisted as though she had tasted something bitter. I was sorry for Luke.

That night I went quietly to the old house. It was bright moonlight. I was afraid that she might have some young tough from Perelkop with her, so I took the Boxer with me and put a revolver in my pocket.

The Greyling was alone. She slept right under the lattice, within reach of a man's arm, but the flimsy door was locked. Her hair was hidden by the pillow and in the moonlight she looked like a White girl.

She awoke suddenly with a cry of "Beloved!" that changed to a whimper of terror when she saw me.

"Don't be frightened, Bokkie. I only looked in to make sure you were alone."

"Missis, I got a fright. Lying here with the moon shining on me . . . Oh my God. The nonna Delport says that if a person sleeps in the moonlight, the moon will pull the face right over like it does the sea to make the tides. She knows of a man who lay sleeping on a ship in the moonlight, and when he woke up his whole face was skew. Is mine still on straight, nonna?"

I could not help laughing, yet I knew that this bright talk of hers was to deceive me: the Greyling was frightened and she had been expecting a lover. She had got out of bed and was standing respectfully at the door. She wore a flannel nightgown that was so long and wide on her that one could almost see Tante's shape still in it.

Something stirred in the rooms beyond where the mealies were stored.

"Nonna, the rats!" Bokkie said. "At first I used to think it was ghosts. I thought Oubaas Van Doorn didn't like me sleeping in his house. But then I saw a rat the size of a dog. I put my panties and stockings under my pillow . . . see." She lifted a corner of the pillow. "A rat will run off with anything soft and fine to make his nest. You should hear them on the roof sometimes, it's a regular rugby match."

"Luke can have another rat hunt."

"If the nonna hears me talking at night, I'm only telling the rats to get away."

"Well, see the rats don't answer you, Bokkie, like one did last night."

She shrieked with laughter, bending at the knees as though the joke were too great to be borne standing erect.

I made her move her bed away from the lattice.

Her lover was Maarten Delport. He came to Banghoek late at night with a torch and shotgun: if anybody saw him, if the dogs betrayed him, he had an excuse for being out so late. There was good shooting on the boundaries and he had permission to come on our land.

I had been to Pretoria to see my husband and I was not due back that night: usually I spent the night at my father's house. But my father and I quarrelled over politics . . . he had recently joined the Progressive Party . . . and I drove back to the farm in the dark. It was eleven o'clock and the house was empty and cold: Raymond was with Mrs. Rottcher who had looked after him since babyhood during my visits to the prison. Japie had taken advantage of my absence to sneak off to Perelkop for the night.

The thought of entering the house oppressed me and I remained outside, taking Samson with me for company. The farm was quiet, there was not so much as the stamp of a beast's hoof or the sigh of a sleeper to be heard; but from the untouched bushveld beyond the farms came the eerie cries of the smaller hunting animals, and once the roar of a lion near Nulsi. The cattle stirred in a ripple of unease and the Boxers stood up out of sleep with rising hair. The silence that followed was dizzying. There might be peace in it for me, I thought, and stopped in my slow pacing at the great rock near Bokkie's room where she and Maarten waited in terror for his chance to leave: they had been asleep for they thought they had the whole night before them. The sound of the car had woken Bokkie first and she put her mouth close to Maarten's ear to whisper to him. He dressed at once, thinking he would be able to slip away when I went inside. So they waited there, listening to my footsteps, first on the terrace and then on the little path to the rock. In the moonlight I saw Foeitog crouching with her nose to the crack of Bokkie's door.

The rock was as cold as a cell wall when I leaned against it. I longed for my son.

I wanted him so much that I rang up Mrs. Rottcher

to tell her that I was coming to fetch him; but she would not hear of this. "Ilse, my poor child. I know what you've been through today. Stay there, I'll wrap him nicely in a blanket and bring him over." Before I could protest, she had rung off.

As soon as he heard me go away from the rock, Maarten was out of Bokkie's room. The faint snap of the lock alerted Samson: he flew down the path to investigate. He knew Maarten and gave him a Boxer's welcome. Maarten was in the middle of the driveway pushing him down when I came out of the house to call Samson in. Maarten had his gun with him and Foeitog was at his heels.

I called out: "Maarten," and he turned his face blindly towards me. "Will you open the gates for me as you go out: Mrs. Rottcher is bringing Raymond back in a few minutes."

He raised his hand and with Foeitog still at his heels walked on. I thought he had come from a hunting jaunt . . . Foeitog would have enjoyed herself. Then I remembered that I had seen Foeitog outside the Greyling's room. I went there and saw the footprints of a man in the soft ground.

Maarten was almost at the gates. I called out to him again: "Come here, Maarten."

I went to meet him.

"Mrs. Van Doorn?"

"You've been in that girl's room."

"Don't be a fool."

I showed him the footprints at Bokkie's door.

"I saw Foeitog outside here a few minutes ago."

He sneered at me. "Go to the police, they'll laugh at you."

"I'll go to Rottcher."

For a moment I was afraid of him standing there with the gun in his hands.

"Rottcher won't need legal proof, Maarten."

Bokkie began to cry.

The headlights of the Rottchers' car shone on us briefly as it topped the rise. Maarten, with an animal's swiftness, ran for the fence and sprang over. Mrs. Rottcher was already at our gates. She saw Maarten standing in the grass.

"Come and open the gates, young Delport, what are you just standing there for? Well, what was the bag tonight?" Her voice came clearly across the stillness.

Behind me the door of Bokkie's room swung open. I felt my hand caught and kissed.

She was whispering, "Nonna, in Christ's name . . . as you love Christ . . . by His blood . . ." When I pushed her away, she caught my dress. "Do it for Jesus Christ . . . his mother, the Oubaas, basie Raymond . . ." She kissed my feet.

I waited until Mrs. Rottcher had gone and Raymond was asleep before I went to her room. By the light of my torch I found her candle and matches. She was standing rigid in the middle of the room. I struck her across the face.

"I should send for the police."

"I'll promise the nonna . . . I'll never do it again. Nonna, help me."

"The nonna Delport helped you."

She shuddered and cried. "I love him. It has not been an easy love. I knew that for him to touch me meant prison for us both. I fear myself as though I were a leper. All along I have said to him, Leave me alone: but he would not. Now he is ruined. Oh, nonna, beat me until I am pulp but don't go to the police or to Baas Rottcher. Nonna, in Christ's name, don't spoil his life." She went down on her knees before me. "It will never be again. I swear it."

"Then pack your things. Get."

Floundering in the long nightgown, she began picking up her things. She made a bundle and then had to undo it again because she needed some clothes to put on.

I gave her the money owing to her and let her go away into the darkness.

Maarten Delport meant to blow out his brains as soon as he saw Rottcher's car or a police car being driven on to Diamant: he was in the old mealie lands where he had a view of the road. He wished that he could write a note to his parents, something to say he was sorry, but he had not the courage to go to the house.

At first he had the company of the dogs which quested round him in the harsh dusty stubble; but as the night grew colder they left him to return to their boxes on the stoep. He was warm enough, for he had worn his overcoat when he went to see the Greyling, and he had a flask of brandy in the pocket.

He had been lying in bed drinking with Bokkie earlier in the evening and two or three swigs from the flask put him to sleep after a while.

The Greylong almost fell over him. She had been cutting across the fields on her way to the house; she meant to tell him that I was not going to Rottcher or the police. When she saw the gun beside him, she thought he was dead; it flashed into her mind that his parents had driven him out of the house to commit suicide and she was cursing them as she bent over him.

He had fallen asleep with his head pillowed on his arms. In the moonlight she could see only the back of his head and his long slender fingers. She sat close to him. I love you, I love you, she said in her mind: O God, work a miracle, make me White . . .

She thought he must be cold lying there and she undid her bundle and spread her clothes over him. Her movements woke him. He brushed off her clothes with a gesture of disgust.

"Sis, what are these?"

"I thought you would catch cold lying there."

"Rottcher . . . Has his car passed while I was asleep? Is he looking for me?"

"Nonna Van Doorn isn't going to tell anybody."

He took a long drink from the brandy bottle.

"I was going to kill myself, Greyie. I was only waiting until I saw the police or Rottcher coming."

"Then I would have killed myself too."

"I was alone here. Even the dogs left me."

"At least I am here now."

"It's hell," he said, lying down beside her. "You must keep away from me, Bokkie, you dirty little bastard. If you ever come near me again, I'll kill you."

He took her, hurting her as he often did. When he was finished with her, he got up and left her without a word.

She gathered her clothes and made up her bundle again. She could hear Maarten's footsteps crackling on the dry stalks. He was almost clear of the field when he turned back. She stood there ready to go on.

"It's cold, Greyie."

"You warmed me, basie," she said.

"Here, finish what's in the bottle."

"You'll make a drunkard of me."

"Get under my coat," he said when she had gulped the brandy.

So he walked a little way with her, yawning.

"You're dead for sleep, basie. I'll go to the hollow and make a little fire, then I'll keep warm."

"Good."

At dawn she passed through the mealie lands again. She could see the patch of broken stalks where she had lain with Maarten during the night. The lands were desolate beneath the pale sky but she remembered them always because she had walked across them with Maarten sharing his coat.

She went to the Storm valley and lived alone in an abandoned shanty. Luke found her there when he returned from seeing his mother. He had quarrelled with his mother who had refused to part with any money but he still hoped to get Bokkie until he saw that she would soon have a child: not even Tante's wide dresses could hide her secret now.

Sipho gave her a bed and planted some mealies for her; he gave her as well two she-goats from the little herd he ran at Diamant. When her time came he sent an old woman to confine her.

If he guessed who the father of her child was he kept it to himself. He was old and he did not want to move from Diamant. His womenfolk were told to keep a curb on their tongues and if they spoke about Bokkie's child at all it was in the privacy of their huts.

CHAPTER 5

Mahomedy's store was in a dusty back street. Not many White people shopped there. Although it was only a few blocks away from the centre of the town, it had a countrified look as though it were a store on the veld, for there was a vacant plot next to it covered with grass and the road was untarred. Fowls scratched on the road and flew on to the stoep, Native women sat on the stamped earth outside as they do at a country store. Across the windows there was splashed the announcement: Summer Clearance Sale, in bright pink phosphorescent paint; for Mahomedy always hoped to attract White custom. He held a perpetual sale. Next week he would in all likelihood be announcing, perhaps in green paint, an End-of-the-Season Sale.

I went down there to buy some cheap blankets for the servants. Maarten Delport was in the shop. Mahomedy was holding up an infant's dress for him to see.

Maarten called across the shop: "Mother's feeling

the heat so I'm shopping for her. She wants to send some things to Cissie."

"She should have asked me."

We spoke to each other only when we had to and I thought nothing of his awkwardness as he hastily finished his shopping and almost ran from the shop.

I called in to see Tante on my way home from Perelkop. The church building party had broken up. Tante had given a farewell dinner for the Bruggemanns to which Raymond and I were invited. The Bruggemanns' pig had been eaten at the dinner. Raymond, with bulging eyes, watched it consumed: I had the foresight to hint to Tante that we did not like pork and we had chicken. Bruggemann now had a steady job in Bloemfontein; Cissie was expecting a child. Kotze was riding up and down the country working on his mission. But Bruggemann's sister Ella was at Diamant. Oubaas had engaged her as a companion to Tante. She was a pretty girl but delicate.

That day we sat in the front room because the kitchen was too hot. Maarten sat next to Ella on the sofa opposite me. Tante was a little jealous. It showed in the pouting of her lower lip and in the sudden twitch she gave to the page of the magazine she was looking at.

Maarten began to wrestle with Ella. They were playing together like young animals. Tant Bertha went out of the room. She was resigned to the fact that Maarten and Ella had paired off, indeed she liked to say to other women: "Martie has got himself a nice girl, you know . . ." but she hated to see Maarten with his hands on the girl.

Tante showed me the baby's dresses that Maarten had bought for her to send to Cissie.

"Why didn't you ask me, Tante, I'd have done it for you and saved Maarten the embarrassment."

"He insisted on doing it. Martie loves to do things for his mother."

That night Maarten came to Banghoek. He entered the house swiftly as I opened the door to him.

"Help me," he said.

"What is it?"

"Where's Raymond? And the servants?"

"Raymond is asleep and the servants have gone."

He came into the sitting-room and shut the door.

"The Greyling has had a child."

"So?"

"Oh help me, there's nobody else I can turn to."

"What do you expect from me?"

"When the child is older, the others will persecute her down there in the valley. I saw what happened to Bokkie."

"Too late to worry about that now."

"No it isn't. If you could help me to get the child adopted into a Coloured family somewhere, perhaps in Natal or the Cape. . . . Then she would have a chance, among people like herself. Bokkie is threatening to move in with her cousins. I tried to persuade her to go away to a city and live among Coloured people but she has turned spiteful. She's got the cheek to talk about us going away together. You want to see her, she's tried to fix herself up to look White. And she has even called the baby Diamant for the whole world to know what I have done. You could persuade her to be sensible. My God, I can't bear to think of that child among the Blacks. In a Coloured family, if she has to suffer anything, it will be what all children suffer . . . from wanting some little thing they can't have or even from a grown-up's bad temper. She won't be half-killed because of the colour of her skin. Help her. I'll tell you everything," he went on recklessly. "When Bokkie went to live in the valley, I visited her occasionally. She was the one then who was always talking about taking the baby to live among Coloured people. The first idea we had was that she should marry Luke. . . .

"The baby was three days old when I saw it. I've paid for what I did. I never thought I could feel like that . . . I'm half-mad with grief when I think of what I'm responsible for.

"Poor little devil. I gave Bokkie money to buy some clothes for the child but she spent the money on herself. That's why I offered to buy Cissie's things, I was able to get an outfit for the child: it was as naked as a Kaffir baby.

"Will you go down and ask that bloody Greyling to leave or to give up the baby to a Coloured family?"

"I don't want to be mixed up in it. It was enough that I kept quiet before. Now this."

"I can do nothing with Bokkie. Help me. In the mood she's in, she's likely to burst in on my mother and say, Here's your grandchild. She has got some mad plan in her head to go White."

He tried to take my hand but I drew away.

"You must think I am filthy."

I said, "For your mother's sake I'll see what I can do with Bokkie," but this was not altogether true: his concern for the child had moved me.

I pitied him. I saw him as a doomed man. Some men express joy in their possession of woman; not only men like old Adraanse who had no ambition except to enter his garden of Eden but men like Rottcher who gloried in his attainments, lands and race.

Rottcher was a simple man who accepted his power as a badge of masterhood. But it seemed to me that Maarten like my husband was more complex and had used his body to express his masterhood; as a feudal lord might have done, or a soldier fresh from battle.

It was not enough for Ray that he was the landowner and Adraanse his bywoner. It was not enough for Maarten that he was White, a first-class citizen, a voter; there were still Adraanse's daughter and the Greyling to lie submissively beneath them.

I met the Greyling under a wild olive tree where she was waiting for Maarten. She was sitting on a striped towel that had been thrown over the dusty dry grass. She had her baby with her. The little girl did not have Bokkie's woolly hair but tiny tight waves close to the scalp with a tinge of gold to them. I saw that Bokkie had used hair-straightener on her own wool and it was like the down of a young bird's wing, not shining, and black without tints of blue or purple. She had used a bleach on her skin which was now creamy and as light as the baby's. Bokkie's eyes were lovely in this blanched face. She had used Maarten's money not only to buy cosmetics but also a tight blue dress that showed the mounds of her body; and a pair of stiletto-heeled shoes in which her thin feet, arched and cramped, looked as though they were drawn up by wire.

She was alarmed at seeing me and stood up defensively.

"Nonna, why have you come?"

"Baas Maarten asked me to help him."

"Oh, nonna, give me hope."

"I can give you hope for the child if you listen to what I say. You must leave here or let the child be adopted."

She arranged the baby's dress which was the one I had seen Maarten buy in Mahomedy's store.

"Martie and I could go away together, one reads about it in the newspaper. To Ghana perhaps, even to England or America. That is why I straightened my hair."

"It is only a dream, Bokkie. I came to speak about the reality."

"Martie loves her." She held the baby out to me as though she wanted me to hold her.

"Not loves but pities," I said without touching the baby.

"And you? Do you pity her?"

"Yes."

"Nobody pities me," she said, stumbling over the words. "When I saw Martie with the baby for the first time, I was surprised, he was so nice with her. He took her on his hands, holding her as though his hands were a tray, it made me laugh. And when he put her down again, he had a look at her toes and fingers. There was a loving expression on his face. Nonna, he has never been nice to me like that, even when we were children. I was always the Coloured. Even the first time . . . God's my witness I was a virgin . . . he broke into me as if he wanted to smash me up for life. And he thrashed me when I told him I was going to have a baby. Do you remember that black eye I had?

"After he found me in the valley here, he often came hunting and he would come late at night and sit on a box in my room paring off biltong and tell me about the hunt. He would give me some of the biltong. If he had shot anything, I'd cook and we would eat together. Once or twice he slept with me, only sleeping, nothing else, because I suddenly got very big. But I must always remember I am a Coloured. If I called him Martie, he wouldn't say anything sometimes, other times he would tell me to shut up and call him Baas. But it is different when he looks at the baby. That first time I cried. I did not know that he could look like that at a Coloured."

"You must make the best of it, Greyie. If it's any comfort to you, he thinks of the child first and foremost as a Coloured. That is in his mind all the time. He wants to save her from unhappiness. Be grateful for that. Now I want you to agree to go away with her or have her adopted by Coloured people."

"She is my grandfather's. I couldn't cheat him. He is entitled to lobolo from me."

"We'll see about the money side. But agree to go or to part with her."

She stood there trying to say something past the anguish gathering in her. From her mumbled words I knew it had to do with the father who had repudiated her, and with Maarten's tenderness for her child. At last I had to take the child for she sank on to the veld. I sat close enough to her to breathe in the muskiness of her grief-sweat; and I said to her that she would find love and peace but I knew that it was beyond the power of anybody human to heal the wound her parents gave her, she must endure as a cripple endures, and trust in God.

"The child will love you one day. Take her and go among your own kind, Bokkie," I said, but for a long time she would not stop crying for what she could not have, Maarten's tenderness.

She talked to me when her grief was subdued and told me about that night with Maarten in the mealie-field, their terror when I came home unexpectedly and her childhood.

The Greyling had suffered, people had clawed at her as though they were wild beasts: not only her body had been torn but the very fabric of her inner being had been mutilated. It only remained now for her to be kicked to death, to be flung into the earth, obliterated, utterly stamped out; or to take a knife to her own throat.

She was once sitting alone when she was eleven years old, not far from the tree where we had met. She was a little woman for the first time that day, and she was just sitting there thinking: I'm Bokkie Sipho. She wished she could step outside herself and have a look. It did not matter then that she was a Coloured living on sufferance in a kraal, she felt elated by this gentle secret whispering of her blood. She knew in a dizzying flash a sense of oneness with females, even with the grand White ladies of Perelkop, with her own arrogant relations and with the low Black tarts who sold them-selves for ninepence at the bus terminus, with bitches and lionesses . . . it was a powerful vision. She belonged in female nature. When she put her hand between her thighs it came away sticky. She was proud of herself and showed an old woman who was passing.

"Better for you if it never happened," said the Black woman, "what can you ever breed but bastards?"

She might have been saved if she had fallen in love with a Coloured boy but it was Maarten she loved. She had been working in his mother's house, running errands, washing Tante's feet, collecting eggs, polishing the furniture, nothing too hard for a child. Tante was kind to her and for a while it was Tant Bertha she loved. She had longed to be called darling or my sweetheart by Tante but that would never be. Tante called her little maid or little creature, and only once, absentmindedly, my child.

Tante advised Sipho to send her to school, she would pay the costs. So when her schooling was done, Bokkie worked at Diamant for a year without wages to pay her debt. She would have worked there for ever for nothing just to see Maarten and because of him she did not go to the city to the good job she had been trained for. Oubaas had agreed to let her go in spite of Sipho owing him money.

"But, nonna, I was in a desert. I was like a cactus in a desert. It seemed to me I was swollen up, hard like a cactus from storing up my love for I was eighteen and had never had a boy."

If Maarten touched her it would ruin him. Love between them was immorality. It meant a crime, prison. Bokkie was afraid. She saw the crime written out big and clear in a newspaper: Maarten Van Oordt Delport, 22, and Bokkie Sipho, 18, were today sentenced in the Perelkop Magistrate's Court for an offence against the Immorality Act on the night of . . . She would have considered going to prison a small price to pay for giving herself to Maarten. But for him it would mean final disgrace, the end of his life.

Maarten began to notice her soon after he came under Rottcher's influence: he was just going on for twenty-one. There was an evening when he came up behind her and said: "Go down to the plantation, Bokkie, and wait by that big old tree." She knew the tree he meant, they had played beneath it when they were children. That was the first time he asked her. She did not go to the plantation then but in the afternoons when she had her time off she used to sit under the tree and imagine what would have happened if she had gone to meet him.

Maarten found her there one afternoon, in the summer. She knew he was coming for she heard him walking on the brittle pine needles. She stood up. He took hold of the top of her dress and pulled it away from her body so that he could look down on her breasts.

"Basie, leave me alone," she whispered, but she was filled with delight and could not move away from him. Some Natives were passing. They were out of sight on the roadway but the sound of them made Maarten drop his hands. They were released from the spell and walked away from each other.

She shared a room with two of her cousins. There came a night when she was alone in the room, the other two girls having gone to sleep at the house of a friend who was to be married the next day. Maarten knew. He got over the fence of the kraal. She had padlocked the door and she would not open it to him: the window was too small for him to climb through. He whispered at the window: "At least let me see you, Bokkie," and she took off her nightgown and came close to the window. He touched her.

The Oubaas was calling in the garden. Maarten lied to him, saying that he had gone to ask Sipho about a sick cow and found him asleep but the Oubaas was suspicious. From that time he encouraged Maarten to think about getting married. He said to him: "If you are desperate, it would be better to go to Plat Anna than to hang about the kraals. At least you don't risk prison, and you are less likely to catch a disease from a White woman."

The next day was Saturday, the day of the wedding; in a backyard near Mahomedy's. Bokkie went there with her people. That night Sipho gave her permission to go to a bioscope to which Coloureds were admitted. The pictures were shown in a hall which had been partitioned to separate Coloureds and Indians from the White people. Maarten was there. He saw her as they left the bioscope but he did not return her greeting.

He was not going straight home. She stood and watched the lorry as it swung round a corner into a dismal lane; Plat Anna lived there. Bokkie knew at once what Maarten was going to do. She was beside herself with grief and jealousy. Plat Anna was White but she was low; like a frog, huge and round, with a frog's downcurving toothless mouth. Living with her was a hard girl she called her cousin, and her sister who was frail and tall, without arms. So shrivelled and ghastly was the face of the sister that her deformity lay in that it seemed and not in the stumps of arms. People said she looked on while the so-called cousin lay with the men who came to the house.

Bokkie ran into the lane, she wanted to cry out to

her beloved to come to her. When she reached the lorry, Maarten had already entered Plat Anna's house. Bokkie crouched next to the front tyre, like a mournful bitch. Presently she saw the armless woman come round from the back on to the stoep and look in through the window: she stood motionless, straight as a wooden carving at first but presently began to roll her hips and to move the stumps of her arms like wings.

The door opened with a jerk and Maarten ran out. He dashed to the lorry. He did not seem surprised to find Bokkie there: it was as though they had made an appointment to meet. "Get in," he said, "but sit on the floor so that nobody sees you."

"Was it the face at the window that frightened you?" Bokkie asked as they rushed through the night.

"I saw no face at the window. Plat Anna's face was enough for me and the face of that girl she called pretty. For a White girl to sink so low . . . she'll burn in hell."

He turned off the lights of the lorry as they entered the Diamant plantation. Bokkie had been thinking of love as it was shown on the bioscope but he took her with a brutal thrust.

She was back with her people only about half an hour late, so quickly was he done with her.

Thereafter she went to the plantation whenever he asked her. She avoided suspicion at home easily because she was the one to light the fire for Tante in the mornings. If she was questioned for roaming about at night, she used to say she had mistaken the time. So she and Maarten were often together.

When they were small, he ten and she eight years old, they met beneath the old tree and began to play together. Presently on the bank of the spruit there appeared a Native woman. She wore a dress which was in rags and a soiled doek. She pulled the doek off her head and fastened it on a thornbush, then the dress came off. The children sat watching without a sound. She could not hang her dress up for it tore on the thorns and they wanted to giggle when she placed it carefully beneath a flat stone. She washed herself. Then she scrubbed at her heels with a pebble. She had only a small piece of soap which she had rubbed on her body and let dry so that she was shining. Her hair had been plaited, there must have been a hundred plaits on her head, with beads fastened on the ends; little snakes, each with a blue eye. She was a fat woman whose flesh quivered as she walked. She went into the bushes. The bushes were thin and they saw a White man waiting for the woman: he must have sent her away to wash. The children saw his buttocks. His buttocks were scarred, he had evidently been given strokes at some time.

The children crept away to the open veld.

Bokkie said: "That's how we were born."

"I wasn't," Maarten shouted. "That's how a Coloured is born . . . you. Now you know why it is terrible to be a Coloured."

"I wish I was Black."

"Listen to this," said Maarten. "It is something my aunt told me. The German Kaiser had some English blood in his veins but he let it out. He opened a vein in his wrist. After that he was a pure German because he let out half his blood. That's what I would do if my blood was half White and half Black."

"I'll let my White blood flow out," said Bokkie. "My grandmother hates me for it."

"The Kaiser's arm withered."

Bokkie had picked up a piece of glass in the veld.

"Do it for me," she said.

"Won't you mind if your arm withers?"

"Not if I get rid of my White blood."

"Why not get rid of your Black blood?" Maarten asked suddenly.

"No. It is my White blood my grandmother hates."

Maarten cut deeply into Bokkie's wrist. The blood came out spurting onto the grass. She might have died if Maarten had not run for help.

They never spoke again of those two whom they had seen in the plantation; but Bokkie remembered them that first time Maarten took her and accepted his brutality as she had accepted that not even a river of blood flowing from her could change the fact that she was a Coloured.

Now she accepted neither his brutality nor her status; she would have his tenderness, she would make herself White.

CHAPTER 6

Maarten drove us in the Rottchers' car to a Republican rally in Welkom; his mother, Tante, the Oubaas, Ella Bruggemann and I were jammed on the seats and Raymond was on the floor. Rottcher had gone ahead with a lorryload of supporters.

The car was a Buick. It was upholstered in grey velvet and there was a soft grey carpet on the floor; a city car, said Tante. She was terrified that Mrs. Rottcher would notice that some red farm mud had been tramped into the carpet by somebody's shoes.

The meeting had been solemn. Before the speeches began, some ladies in Voortrekker costume had pinned a carnation on the lapels of each dignitary on the platform. Mrs. Rottcher, on the way home, wanted to talk about the meeting but Tante was tired of politics. She persisted in changing the conversation and Mrs. Rottcher lapsed into an ominous silence.

"Riding in this car is better than flying," said Tante. "I remember that when I flew in an aeroplane to Durban that time I felt as if the thing was suspended by a thread from the sky."

Ella giggled.

"At dusk you can't feel the wheels on the road," Tante went on, "it seems to me then that the road unwinds like a spool beneath you. . . ."

"It's not dusk now, Tante, it's ten o'clock in the morning," said Ella.

"I'm well aware of that. How this car is straining towards the hills. It wants to leave the Free State." Ella was a Free Stater.

Oubaas was anxious to make a match between Ella and his son. He cut in hastily: "There is something attractive about the Free State all the same."

"Attractive!" cried Tante; indeed the country through which we were passing then was only thinly covered with grass. What rivers there were wound like snakes across the land.

"I mean the girls, not the scenery," said the Oubaas.

Ella pouted and giggled.

Tante would just as soon have quarrelled with her. "I do not like the Free State."

At last, to our relief, Mrs. Rottcher spoke: "We should love every part of our dear Republic to be." After that she had her way and talked politics.

On flew the car to our distant hills. We came to populated areas. There were houses and trains and the tarmac road with flashing cars on it. Our car was unknown and only part of all the traffic until we left the main road for the district road. Now the familiar dust seeped in although we closed the windows, and the car that had been so steady rocked slightly on the rough road.

It was known here. Native children ran to open the gates: Mrs. Rottcher gave them a handful of boiled sweets which she kept in the glove box for the purpose. Already we were at the signpost: Banghoek R. Van Doorn.

Mrs. Rottcher sat up straight as old Van Doorn's monument came into view. We all stared respectfully at that admonishing finger pointing to the sky.

Just beyond stood the Greyling with her child.

She came up the hill slowly in her high-heeled shoes, and the car had raced on by the time she had reached the house. I had gone in to wash and change. I came outside again to find her sitting on the lawn with her shoes off. She had a small suitcase with her.

"Well, what have you decided to do?"

"Was the young nonna Bruggemann sitting next to him?" she said but cringed as she spoke.

"Be careful."

There were servants in the house. I made her move away towards the big rock near her old room: Raymond was playing with Samson, glad to be free after the cramped ride.

"It was that Bruggemann girl."

"Don't dare talk like that. Tell me what you have decided to do."

"I can't bear to think of him with her."

"Have you gone mad? You have no claim on Baas Maarten except for some money. You must try not to be wicked. You will ruin yourself and him if you go on like this."

She began to cry. I thought I had subdued her and waited for her to calm herself.

She said, "There is a man in the valley, he is in politics. He said White men often go away with their Coloured sweethearts and marry them outside. There is nothing to prevent Martie from taking me away. This man says he knows a secret route."

"Who is he? I'll report him to the police."

"He has gone away, nonna."

"Have you told him who the father of your child is, you wicked creature?"

"No, I only spoke in a general way."

"Listen, Bokkie. Maarten Delport remains your baas in spite of what has happened. He has no wish to go anywhere with you. Understand, you mean nothing to him. Nothing, nothing. All he is thinking of, all I am thinking of, is to help your child."

"You could see the little nonna's hair shining like the sun."

"Shut up. Are you going away?"

"I thought of it. I've got my things in this suitcase. But I can't go, nonna. I've never been anywhere else in my life but here. I'm frightened to go away alone. And who is to look after my child?"

"Find a foster-mother for her."

She walked away, still crying. Late in the night she was still crying somewhere on the veld. She set all the dogs barking for miles around. Luke went out and got her and the child. She would not come into his shack but shivered on a corner of his stoep until dawn, then she went away again.

At five in the afternoon she presented herself at Diamant and asked Tante for her old job back. Her child she had sent to her cousins in the Storm valley. Tante was only too glad to take her on since there were twenty-three people sitting down to supper that evening. She was under the impression that Bokkie was still engaged to Luke and only waiting for the mother's consent before getting married.

Oubaas it was who had set her off on a whirl of entertaining: he was out to prove to Ella that life on Diamant was a round of pleasure. Supper was served at a big oval table. The vegetables were brought in in huge dishes carried round by the servant. Maarten suddenly put down his knife and fork. I had seen only the hands on the bowl of vegetables, slender hands that had been bleached from their original brownness. They were yellowish now, with a tracery of lilac veining that made them look fragile. I did not connect them with the Greyling until I saw Maarten's breakdown. He sat there motionless, still as a person I had once seen drifting on the aura of an epileptic fit. I looked up at the Greyling. She was serving peas deftly, her face insolent beneath a white doek that Tante had made her wear.

Ella leaned towards Maarten anxiously.

"Are you ill?"

He could not answer her. Ella refused the peas as though she were afraid that he had found a worm in them. She stared after the Greyling who was on her way out of the room. The Oubaas got up suddenly and followed the Greyling.

"His cough troubles him," Tante said.

The Oubaas came back. He was breathing heavily as a man might do after a fit of coughing.

"Just give me the subject," he said, adjusting his hearing aid.

"We were talking about Italy," I said.

"The land of spaghetti." To make us laugh the Oubaas rolled out the g with a guttural sound.

Maarten was recovering himself. The Greyling had not come back into the dining-room.

"Pieter chased Greyie," Tante whispered to me after an excursion to the kitchen to find out what had happened to the girl. She was downcast; she had been pleased to have Bokkie working for her again.

Oubaas had taken Bokkie by the shoulders and run her out of the house. He had distrusted her for a long time yet he dared not breathe a word of his suspicions to his son, much less his wife. To deal such a blow to his wife . . . it was beyond him. And Maarten was on the verge of proposing to Ella: he dared not risk a quarrel with him. If Sipho had not owed him so much money he would have sacked him there and then, and got rid of the whole family.

During the night Bokkie climbed through the window into the room where Ella was sleeping. Ella's hair was unbound, long enough to lie on her shoulders. Bokkie saw her by the light of a small lamp on the bedside table: Ella often had attacks of breathlessness and needed the pills that stood by the lamp ready to her hand. Bokkie knelt down and looked at the girl, so close that their breath mingled.

Ella slept on while Bokkie examined her and fixed in her memory the exact shades of her skin and hair, even of the thread-like veins in her temples; she saw not the shape of the girl but her colour. A sob was beginning in her, so deep inside that it was in her bowels. Now she understood that the hair straightener and the bleaching cream were useless. In that room she gave up the idea of trying to make herself White, as she had once given up the idea of making herself Black.

She moved away from Ella. She had touched nothing

since entering the room but now stroked the hard bright ribbon on Ella's petticoat which was flung over the back of a chair: Ella wore dresses with wide skirts and tight bodices over brilliant stiff petticoats. Bokkie's hands grew rough.

Ella woke and screamed. The Greyling was out of the room at once.

Maarten snatched up his shotgun and a torch. He did not shoot when he recognized Bokkie running through the gates. He threw aside the gun but continued to chase her. Bokkie ran on into the veld and hid in a donga while Maarten searched for her. He could not find her.

She crept to Luke's door. She let him take her in this time; she was shivering and afraid. Luke sat with her giving her hot drinks and aspirin, but at four o'clock he realized that she was seriously ill and sent for me: she had begun to rave. It was uncanny to see her. She held her hands before her and squeezed the air as though she squeezed a throat, she tore from a head invisible to us long strands of hair: she was crying harshly like a bird. Perhaps this sound she was making brought back a memory of the veld for she raised herself on her elbow and pointed at some brown birds that she could see rising from the floor to the ceiling and drifting down again on purple-tipped wings.

She was taken to Perelkop hospital and lay there for three weeks, suffering from pneumonia. Tante put her behaviour down to her illness and sent her presents while she was in the hospital.

The Delports and Ella went to Jakkalspan. From there they were to go to Bloemfontein to hear the Prime Minister speak but before they left the Oubaas made a cautious statement to the police about the Greyling's entry into the house. He laid no charge but a policeman called on her in the hospital and gave her a warning.

When she was discharged, she came to me to say thank you for visiting her and for bringing presents.

"I was at Diamant to say thanks for this but they have gone away," she said, smoothing a yellow jersey she wore. "See, it is not the nonna's. I know whose it is."

"The nonna's jerseys would go round you three times now instead of twice, Bokkie."

"It shows a kind heart," she said, not smiling at my joke. "She must be nice, that young lady, to give up her jersey to a person she hardly knows. When I looked at her that night, I thought she was good. . . ."

I was planting out some seedlings. She kicked off her shoes and helped me. All afternoon she worked beside me. Twice she told about her visit to Ella's room: the girl haunted her.

I said at last: "Will nothing cure you, Bokkie? You nearly died. God sometimes makes us sick to stop us in our tracks so that we can take another direction. Sink yourself in your baby. Believe me, that is your salvation. That is how I have lived all these years, in my child. What have you decided to do, keep her in the Storm valley to grow up in misery?"

"Luke will marry me. We spoke about it while I was in hospital."

"Surely he will not take the child?"

"Yes, he will, nonna. I want to go away but he is frightened to ask you."

"He can go."

"Baas Maarten need not be frightened of me any more. I will let him be happy. Oh, nonna, don't be angry when I say I love him. I love him and I will never hurt him. I am like a person who has been mad. That night when I served at the table, I was going to tell all those people that he had a child hidden in the Storm valley. So many thoughts I had. I longed for the Bantu to rise up and sweep everything away. I longed for the rape and the death of that White girl. But it is finished now. There will be peace for the basie, for her, for her parents, all of us. I will be good to Luke."

"That's a good girl, Bokkie."

The banns were put up at the Mission church. Bokkie came to live in her old room with the child. Sipho was making difficulties; he demanded the custody of the child until Bokkie's lobolo was paid. Bokkie managed to smooth him over with promises of an early settlement. Every night she wrote a letter in Luke's name, demanding his savings from his mother. All the old woman did was to tear the letters up and post them back to Luke.

I drove up to Jakkalspan to spend the day with the Delports but I did not see Maarten until late in the afternoon as he had taken Ella to the station about twenty miles away: she was going to her brother in Bloemfontein.

"A bit of strategy," said Tante, complacently kneading a lump of clay. "Maarten hasn't asked her yet and I think she has worked it out that a few days' separation will bring him up to scratch. There was this sudden violent longing to go to her little brother though we shall all be going to Bloemfontein on Friday, only three days to wait. But she is giving Maarten a bit of time to think things over and she is sure of seeing him soon before anybody else can make eyes at him. Absence makes the heart grow fonder, the English say."

Tante was laughing but the Oubaas looked serious.

"I never saw a young man hang fire like Martie. He will look silly if the girl finds somebody else in Bloemfontein."

"No fear of that," said Tante. "She's mad about the poor boy."

Oubaas had come in only for his midday meal: diamond-fever had him in its grip again. They had washed the day before and found three small diamonds, now he was living for the next Friday to see what would turn up. He stood over the boys like a slave-driver.

Tante had made an oasis in the dust and noise of the diggings. She had had flooring-boards put down and engaged a little Native boy whom she nagged all day to water the ground outside so that the dust would be laid: there was a hula-hoop festooned with a canary creeper in the tent and some ferns which she made the boy sprinkle from time to time. Frequently she leaned over and dabbed me with eau de cologne. She wanted me to stay and see the model finished: it was to be a head of President Kruger. But I had to leave early because I wanted to meet Maarten coming back from the station so that I could speak to him alone.

It was good to be on the highveld again. I drew up alongside the road to wait for him. There was only grass here and a straight road and the white-hot sky. I wished at first that I could stay here to see the sunset but it was not long before I began to think of Mission Falls and I was glad enough when Maarten appeared.

He got into the car next to me.

"I've brought good news, Maarten. The Greyling is going to marry Luke and they are keeping the child if she can get lobolo for Sipho. They are leaving the district."

"So it's finished at last?"

"Have you got sixty-five pounds? For Sipho?"

"Yes."

"If you give it to me, I'll pretend that I'm lending it to Luke."

"O.K. But I won't be able to get it this afternoon, it's too late. They'll have to wire for it. I'll send it to-morrow or the next day. God, to get myself clear . . . I'd go over broken glass for you, Mrs. Van Doorn."

He would have put his arms round me, I think he wanted to kiss me in gratitude. I pushed him away.

He covered his eyes with his hand.

"You think I'm dirty because of Bokkie." He looked at me, flinging down his hand with a violent gesture. "What about Ella? When I kiss her, do I dirty her too?"

It was true, I had never liked him to touch me since I found him with Bokkie.

I said, "You can't hurt Ella if she doesn't know and if you love her."

"I wish you would let me kiss you."

"Would that wipe out everything of the past?"

"It might wipe out Bokkie's face. I see her some-times even when I kiss my mother."

I turned my lips to his. He kissed me twice, gently, without desire, and watched to see if I would rub my lips.

He did not post the money but brought it to Bang-hoek himself on Friday. Work on the diggings was at a standstill for the Natives had struck and most of them were in gaol. Oubaas and Tante had left early for Bloemfontein. Maarten had told them that he was spending a night or two with friends on the diggings and had then hitched a lift to Perelkop.

He was a little drunk and slapped the money down on the table: I was having coffee on the terrace.

"When I think of the money that old swine of a Sipho owes my father I grudge paying him," he said but he was laughing.

"Be quiet, the maid will hear you."

"Mrs. Van Doorn, little sugar-bush, I could take your hands and do a tickey-draai. I rang up Ella and proposed. She said yes. Surprise. I've bought her a ring and now I'm cleaned out, not a penny in the bank."

While I was looking at the ring, the Greyling came out of her room with her baby on her hip. She stood by the big rock.

"Tell her to voetsak," said Maarten savagely.

She heard him and ran away.

Maarten stayed to supper. He was going on to Bloemfontein that night and borrowed a torch from me as he had to walk through the plantation to the main road to pick up a lift. I would have driven him to the road but I could not leave the house: I was expecting a telephone call from Raymond who was spending the weekend with my father.

The telephone rang as Maarten reached the plantation. Just before I went inside I saw the flash of the torch I had lent him.

CHAPTER 7

A shadow fell on the table while I was bottling honey in the bee-room. I smelt the sharp tang of dagga and of woodsmoke and I thought a Native was standing in the doorway. Without looking round, I said: "Funani?" and fear pierced me because I was trapped in the bee-room which is some distance from the house behind a high fence screening the hives. I was alone on the farm and Samson was shut in his run with a bitch.

"What made you think I was a Kaffir?" said Luke.

I turned slowly to face him, still holding the honey scraper. He was drunk. It is useless to reason with a person who is drunk on dagga so I ignored his insolence and turned to go on with my work though a tremor had started within me, not as yet in my hands or lips, still only a threat to my whole body.

"What made you think I was a Kaffir?" he said again.

"It was just that I wasn't expecting you here. I thought you had gone into Perelkop to meet Bokkie."

"Bokkie is dead." I turned again to look at him.

"Come with me now and see what he did to Bokkie."

He stood aside for me to walk through the doorway. He was so close behind me that I could feel his breath in my hair. I had kept hold of the honey scraper but now the tremor that had started when I knew that Luke was drunk became a part of all my flesh and I would not have been able to lift my shaking hand if he had touched me.

We came out from among the neat rows of hives on to the lawn sloping up to the house. Nobody was about for this was a Saturday afternoon and the servants were at a wedding and the convicts working a few miles off in our plantation under Rottcher's supervision. I looked towards Samson's run but Luke steered me away from it.

I did not feel so frightened once we were on the road for I felt sure that we would meet somebody. But the road was empty all the way to the Delports' plantation where Luke was taking me.

The Greyling was lying across a bush that had broken beneath her weight but still held her in a thorny embrace. She had been strangled. Her tongue was a long black thing pushed out of her mouth. Ants were walking on her eyeballs and there were flies on her, round her lips and stuck to the corners of her eyes. Her body was fixed and rigid except for her hair, the hair like the wing of a bird, which floated in the slight breeze stirring beneath the pines. Luke brushed the ants and flies from her and put his handkerchief over her face.

It was late afternoon and the sun lit only the trunks of the trees; the weeds and long-stranded grass where insects sang lay in shadow. Luke and I sat down. There was sunlight on him. His nose, like pigskin, was a stud in the crimson mask of his face, but his mouth was curved and pink, tucked up firmly at the corners like a child's mouth: his unsteady irises floated in whites that were tinged with some of their brown. He breathed quickly from the effects of the dagga he had smoked and he could not sit still for long but thrust out his legs, beating the ground with his heels in an agony of restlessness. During one of these bouts he leaned over and took the honey scraper from me.

"Where is the baby, Luke?"

"She was not here with Bokkie. He will know what happened to her. After Bokkie saw him yesterday, she came to me and said that she would not marry me. She said it in front of two boys who were waiting for their rations. I went to see her later during the night but her room was locked. I thought I'd leave her alone and she would get over it. You realize I knew all along who was the father of her child but I said nothing for Bokkie's sake.

"I had too much to do to go and see Bokkie early this morning and it was nearly ten o'clock when I went there. Once again the door was locked and a piece of stuff she has put up for a curtain was over the lattice. I thought she must have gone to Perelkop. She goes in on Saturdays to do her shopping and then I meet her and take her to the bioscope. A little Native girl looks after the baby. This little girl hung round until ten: she had arranged with Bokkie to take the baby to the wedding while Bokkie was in town. I thought that Bokkie must have decided that the baby would be neglected at the wedding so I told the girl to go, Bokkie was in town, I said.

"Bokkie was not at our meeting-place. I waited at the bioscope and when she didn't come I went to the kraal where the wedding is taking place. Nobody had seen her today. But one of her cousins said that when she was gathering firewood yesterday afternoon about sunset, she saw Bokkie with her baby sitting in this spot. So I came here and found her. I know who killed her. You know too but will you say so?"

"Yes, Luke. Trust me."

"The police will say I killed Bokkie."

It was growing dark in the plantation. Rain began to fall. Luke removed his shirt and laid it over Bokkie.

"Nonna, I've had bad thoughts," he said, holding his face up to the rain.

"Why do you want to hurt me, Luke?"

"I don't know, nonna. I want to hurt somebody." He shook his head like a confused beast. "When I saw Bokkie lying here, I wanted to hurt somebody but my knees grew weak. So I went to my room and smoked some dagga I took from one of the boys. After that I was strong. I was going to hurt you badly, nonna, you know what I mean. . . ." He stood up. "I'm going to move her off that bush."

"Don't, Luke. The police will punish you."

"They're going to arrest me anyway. I must take Bokkie off the thorns." He tried to pick her up but the thorns held on to her like claws. It looked as if he was wrestling with her corpse.

"Leave her, Luke, she feels nothing."

I began to cry. Luke stopped then.

"You go away, nonna."

"All right, Luke."

I groped a way through the trees. The rain was falling too softly. I wished it would come down hard so that I need not hear Luke tearing Bokkie loose from the thorns and moaning, "Ag come on, Bok, ah Christ, my lamb . . ."

I wanted to run but I went slowly, feeling for the antbear holes that were so numerous here. Only once I fell, crashing against a tree and bruising the side of my face. The going was easier when I reached the road though it was pitch dark now.

Luke joined me. He was smoking a dagga cigarette.

"Go in and telephone the police," he said when we came to the house. He stood on the terrace looking in at the window: the phone was on the other side of the room. My first thought was to lock the doors and windows against him but I realized that he would be inside before I had a chance to bolt the first one. There was a loaded revolver in my bedroom. By the time I ran up the steps to get it, he would have grabbed me. So I crossed at once to the phone and turned the handle. The operator took a long time to answer. I leaned against the wall and watched Luke. He had begun to walk up and down, still smoking. Then he passed out of sight.

I heard a door close at the back. Luke was in the house. I screamed down the receiver but still the operator did not answer. Luke stood next to me but he did not touch me.

"Put the phone back," he said. I was afraid that he would touch me if I did not obey him and I hung the receiver up.

Luke said: "I've thought of something. Don't tell the police I found Bokkie. Say you found her."

"But, Luke . . ."

"You say that, nonna."

"If you've done anything wrong, you're only making it worse for yourself, and if you did nothing to her, why are you acting like this?"

He snarled suddenly: "You know who killed her but will you say so? Tell them you found her. If they know I found her, they'll say I did it."

I picked up the telephone again. The senselessness of what Luke had asked me to do appalled me: did he think of murdering me and making it look as if I had killed Bokkie?

Before the operator answered, Luke told me to put the telephone down again.

"What's the good of that? As soon as they come, you'll tell them the truth. The truth is what they want. Nonna, you tell them that Baas Maarten is the father of Bokkie's child, tell them he was here last night."

"I'll tell them later."

"Say it while I am listening to you."

He came closer to me. I thought, If he touches me I'll faint; but he kept from touching me though by no more than the edge of a knife.

"Pick up the phone, nonna. Say it."

"Even if I do say it, Luke, it does not mean that they will accuse him. He had no reason to hurt Bokkie, he was free of her. . . ."

"They will say Luke had more reason because she had refused him, is that what you mean, nonna? That is what they are sure to say unless they know who fathered her child. You tell them, nonna, it's my only chance." He put his hand close to my throat: I saw his intention in his eyes.

"Leave me alone, Luke. I will tell them." I said to

the sergeant in Perelkop: "Please come, it's Mrs. Van Doorn speaking. A Coloured girl has been murdered in the Delports' plantation. She had a child by Maarten Delport and he was here last night."

Luke moved away from me.

"I am going to find Bokkie's child now, nonna."

Luke went to Diamant to look for Bokkie's child. The kitchen window had been forced and he was able to enter the house. Nobody was there. He could think of only one other place where Maarten would go: Bokkie's shanty in the valley.

Maarten was there asleep with the baby in a box near him. A candle was burning. Luke entered noiselessly. He hoped to take the baby without waking Maarten for he was afraid in spite of the dagga he had smoked: Maarten slept with his hand on a shotgun. Luke had only a knife. Afraid of his own shadow that moved in the candlelight, he stole towards the box: he laid his shaking hands on the baby.

Maarten awoke suddenly and Luke was upon him before he could move. The knife ground against Maarten's breastbone. Luke was sick.

When he looked at Maarten again, he saw that he was still alive. God look after him, he prayed: he was more sober now. Closing his eyes, he tried to staunch the blood with a rag, then he took the child and came to Banghoek.

The police had left a guard on the farm but Luke got as far as the house. He gave the little Diamant to me before he was arrested.

By morning Maarten Delport was in Perelkop hospital under a police guard; and Mrs. Rottcher was at Banghoek.

"But why didn't you call on us for help at once?" she said as she drank coffee.

"The police were here all night. I wasn't afraid."

"I would have thought . . . well, didn't you need a woman's company? It must have been a shock to you. The sergeant rang up my son and told him what had happened. We can't believe that Maarten did a thing like that, it must be the Coloured boy."

"I think so too."

"What's this I hear about a Coloured child?"

"Luke brought her here last night. Mieta is nursing her: she's my washgirl. The sergeant said that Maarten had tried to give the child goat's milk but she was exhausted when I got her."

"You must try and keep clear of all this, my dear. It's going to be very unpleasant if what I hear is true, that the child is Maarten's."

"It is true. And I can't keep clear of it because I will have to give evidence. I had to tell the police that it was Maarten's child."

"Did you know all along then?"

"Yes. Maarten asked me to arrange for the child to be adopted by Coloureds or to get poor little Bokkie away from her Black relations."

Mrs. Rottcher had eyes the colour of those grey pebbles you find on the river bank. By contrast she had a soft, wide-lipped mouth which must have been pretty in her youth but was now heavy, weighing down her chin. At the corner of her lower lip there was a mole sprouting grossly: somehow it gave to her face a look of power. It made me feel afraid of her.

"For how long did you know about Maarten's affair with the Greyling?"

"For quite a while, not from the very start. I caught him here one night."

"It was your duty to report them," Mrs. Rottcher said.

"I thought of his mother."

"If you hide a crime, you condone it and you are guilty of it."

"I drove Bokkie away from here the moment I found out. And once the child was born, I felt sorry for Maarten. He was remorseful."

"He and the girl should have been punished, then there would have been no murder done. Why did you not come to me? My son would have dealt with them if we had considered it necessary to hush the matter up. The laws of our land are founded on God's laws. Does that mean nothing to you?"

"I would have destroyed them all if I had spoken. Have pity."

"Pity? You dare to speak to me about pity. Think back, Ilse, who was it took you in and sheltered you?"

"I know what I owe you. And I was hoping that you would help Tant Bertha in the same way. . . ."

She put down her coffee cup with a gesture of such finality that I felt she would never drink coffee with me again.

"I to help Bertha Delport? How?"

"If Maarten does come to trial . . . if they don't accuse Luke . . . Give Tante your support, then others will rally to her. If there is public sympathy, things won't go so hard with them."

"But what are you talking about?"

I wished I could conquer my fear of her.

"When Ray stood trial, it helped to feel that people

117

were on his side. You must remember how almost everybody was for him, first in this district, from your efforts, and in the end throughout the country. And you helped so much when Raymond and I came to live here. . . ."

"Do you wish me to continue to help you, my child?"

She waited until I answered, as a servant would have to answer: "Yes I do."

"Well, here is my advice. A person in your position, without a husband by her side and with such a scandal on her own doorstep should always act in such a way as to show that she is not a rebel but the victim of circumstances."

"I cannot avoid giving evidence."

"Try as far as possible to hide the fact that you had known for months that a White man had been lying on top of a Coloured girl. Do you hear?" A fleck of foam had appeared beside the mole, and the pebbles of her eyes were warmed by the blood firing her face. "What sort of person are you really, to have shielded them? You answer me, Ilse. Why did you do it? Answer me." I stood numbed before her: this was a bitter taste of the power that had shielded me up to now.

"I sent Bokkie away as soon as I found out."

"But you continued to associate with that filth Maarten, you said nothing. You allowed him to come into my house, touch my hand . . . He used to kiss me."

"I did it for his parents' sake and for Bokkie."

"People like you interest me. Tell me, did you feel no disgust? How could you go to the Delports' house and eat at the same table, perhaps you would have had to touch Maarten's hand and how did you know where he had been putting it previously?"

118

"Maarten had finished with Bokkie, he was going to be engaged to Ella Bruggemann."

"You're far gone, Ilse," saaid Mrs. Rottcher, dry now. "You were willing to allow that innocent Afrikaans girl to become involved with filth like Maarten Delport."

"I remembered what Ray had suffered," I cried.

"Father of pity, Hester Adraanse was a White girl. Ray was different from a man who has had a Coloured girl. God forgive you."

I seemed to be paralysed by her stare. She looked at me; then at the photographs of my son and husband and even at the Boxer that had been growling a little at the passion in her voice. I felt that she was putting a curse on me and on all that belonged to me.

She spoke once more before she left me: "At least get rid of his bastard."

Luke had judged me well. If he had not forced me to speak, I would have continued to shield Maarten. Luke knew that I was afraid of the Rottchers.

He knew something of their power, I knew all of it. You might be speaking to a railway porter and find he owed his job to Rottcher's influence. There were members of the Veld Guard on the church committee, in the school; in the prison.

Ray was due for a remission of sentence. A bad report from a warder, a paper put before an unsympathetic official . . . He might find himself victimized.

At school the seniors might withdraw their protection from Raymond or a master become suddenly harsh . . . At least I could so something for Raymond. I sent him to my father the next day.

As soon as the Delports came back to Diamant, I went to see Tante.

"She will see nobody but the minister," the Oubaas told me.

"Then it is not because I had to tell the police about Maarten and the Greyling?"

"To a certain extent. Why didn't you come to us as soon as you found out?"

"What would you have done?" I said bitterly.

"Moved away . . . anything. If Maarten hadn't been so ashamed . . . I keep going over it in my mind and blaming myself. There should have been more confidence between us. I was too old to be his friend."

"But you guessed there was something between them."

"I am to blame. I saw and pretended not to see. All the time I was thinking of Bertha."

"Speak to her for me, Oubaas. I would still have said nothing if Luke had not forced me."

"You know that they have charged Maarten with murder and that damned Coloured gets off with a thrashing. He is their star witness, I believe."

"I know. But what I came to say really was that I will give evidence for Maarten. If he killed her, it must have been because of an uncontrollable impulse. He was free of her when he left me. Here is the money he gave me for Sipho."

The Oubaas let the notes flutter to the ground between us.

"He will get off, Oubaas. I will tell them everything, how he tried to help the child and never thought of hurting Bokkie even when she was a threat to him after the baby was born. I will tell them in Court how he bought a dress for his child in Mahomedy's shop. Only think what my husband did and he got off with his life."

"God knows we need your help," the Oubaas said and took my hand. "I'll make it right between Bertha and you."

CHAPTER 8

My father and I used to live on a farm near the Crocodile River. The veld sweeps in one pure line to the river bank. In the bushveld you are hemmed in by trees and high krantzes but there your view is un-impeded as far as the horizon. You see not the distant mountains, only the bloom on them. You live with the sky.

My mother died when I was born and I was left with the nuns at Boksburg until I was sixteen.

Ours was in fact not a rural life, the land being in the nature of a hobby to my father: he was a writer, famous only in South Africa for he used Afrikaans. His politics were moderate and he had friends among all sections of the community.

Johannesburg was only twenty miles away and my father was generous. I had lovely clothes, many books; and two Boxers, Samson's parents, to occupy me. There was the companionship of my father and his friends. Yet I remember that I was bitterly unhappy sometimes; every friend that I had, girl or boy, my father took from me by his witty criticisms.

At twenty-one I was lonely. I felt that I was lost, only a mark on the vast plateau beneath the sky.

I used to ride across the veld to exercise the Boxers. Often I went to Mission Falls. Ray had inherited the property from an uncle and I met him soon after he came to look the place over. We were in love at once but I kept Ray from meeting my father. I knew how he would appear in my father's eyes: as bone and muscle and a handsome face; as a Bible-banging exploiter of the Natives. . . .

A bywoner Jocchem Adraanse lived on the farm. His wife had asked for permission to move into the big house when Ray's uncle died, but Ray refused for he did not intend to appoint Adraanse manager. He was looking for a more suitable man. He kept the house shut up and the Adraanses lived in a four-roomed shack near the river.

Adraanse was married to a hefty woman who had given him eighteen children; a small natty man. He used to wear patent leather shoes on the veld. My father said that he must have hook-worm because he would stand for hours doing nothing, apparently vacant.

But I knew he was not vacant. His mind teemed with visions of love, money and perfect health.

"You know, niggie, what I saw last night?" he said to me early one morning: I was giving the dogs a breather before riding home.

"What was it, oom?"

"A tall Indian. Now he had a head, now he didn't. He was standing there under that willow tree over there. Jocchem, he said. How do you know my name? I asked. I know everything, says the Indian. There's a big treasure for you, I'll come back and tell you in two weeks' time. Then he was gone. I could only see the willow tree. Man miss, I've seen some strange things. I saw a cat in the air once, standing up like you and me but in the air, and it shit, that's how real it was. Go to the Coloured herbalist in Jeppestown, it said, you'll be cured of your rheumatism. So I was until the herbalist died. I've tried to see that cat again but it's obstinate. So I suffer." Adraanse was lost in the contemplation of a knotted fist.

I mounted my horse. He smiled at me, showing one rotting fang.

"English Jims! You're pretty up there, niggie. If I were a younger man . . . You've got two pearls of great price under that silk blouse of yours. I can see them shining like two big genuine pearls."

"Sis, oom."

"Sis! Two pearls so big a man could hold them in his hands? Are you ashamed of your breasts?"

"I'll make the dogs bite you."

"You're ashamed. Only think of it. If you're ashamed you will never enter the garden of Eden. It's here with us still but only the naked lovers and the little children enter it. Remember, shame keeps you out. Ask my wife, I've taken her into the garden of Eden how many times? thousands. I'll take any woman in there who wants to go. . . ."

As I rode away, I saw his children everywhere, half-naked little boys, and girls with dresses too long or too short for them; only the youngest were on the farm, the rest had gone to work. His wife, a huge body with a tiny head stuck on top of it, was wringing out a blanket, she at one end and a Native woman at the other.

"From daylight to dark I'm at it," she yelled to me in passing. I said to Adraanse: "You wouldn't be so keen on it if you had to do the work."

Their daughter Hester was an assistant at Caro's holiday resort a few miles along the road. I did not ever see her though I once heard her speaking.

My father and I had gone to Caro's one Sunday afternoon for tea. When we had finished, we sat on the river bank waiting for the park to empty and the dust to settle before driving home.

Hester Adraanse was saying: "If I don't see him soon, I'll kill myself, Sara."

"Ag, Miss Hester, he is sure to come."

She must have been walking with a servant among the willows near us. We heard no more words, only the murmur of her voice. I can recall her voice now. It was undisciplined and would grow hoarse if she were shy or frightened.

"I wonder who it was," I said to my father when we moved away.

"I know a girl Hester who works here. I've bought cigarettes from her when she's been on duty at the kiosk."

"What is she like, Pa?"

"Well, I didn't notice. Dark, I think. Ordinary, not pretty. She is the daughter of old Adraanse."

I saw a newspaper photograph of Hester, after she was dead. She had a heavy face and dark hair and a thick neck; she looked as if she would have big legs and a wide bottom. Yet there was something of my little friend Adraanse in her face, a clouded expression as though she too saw visions.

A few weeks later I told my father that Ray and I were engaged. It began almost at once, the whittling away process; he tried to demolish Ray through his friends, particularly the Rottchers. He satirized them in a story and he even descended to giving a humorous impression of Mrs. Rottcher. It was as though he held up a mirror for me to view Ray.

I needed to be bound to Ray quickly but he was careful in his behaviour to me; it seemed strange that he did not catch fire from me. My father was talking of a trip overseas that June.

Suddenly in March Ray took me. He was insatiable and by May I knew I was pregnant.

It was in March that he had received the first letter from Hester Adraanse. She was living in Johannesburg then for the owner of the resort had dismissed her because she too was pregnant. Ray had got rid of her father; he was working on the roads as a ganger.

She wrote three letters in all. First she threatened suicide and then she threatened to tell me that she was carrying his child. Ray did not answer any of the letters. In the third letter she wrote that she was coming to the farm to see me on May 16th. Ray met every train that day from eight o'clock until she arrived at eleven.

The stationmaster who saw her at our station said she was wearing a navy-blue coat and a grubby headscarf. He said that her whole appearance was untidy. Her face was sallow, without make-up on it. Ray was parked on the road opposite the station. When she saw him, Hester became excited and spilled the contents of her handbag on the platform: she was trying to get a lipstick out. She made up her face quickly before she hurried to meet Ray.

A youth idling on the pavement saw her get into Ray's car. He heard her say: "At last, Ray darling. Oh God, honey, I've missed you." "I've missed you too," Ray said. "We'll go somewhere and talk." "Caro's?" "No, not there, the place is shut up. We'll go to the falls." "Jesus, I've got some memories of that place. And you?"

They drove away. It was true, Caro's was closed for the winter. The road to the falls was dusty and the grass was brown and dry; there was scarcely any water coming over the falls into the muddy pool beneath. The place was deserted.

Ray asked Hester how much she wanted. He could not believe that she was not to be bought off, that she had any real hope that he would marry her, Adraanse's daughter. She cried and he sat there stolidly until she was quiet again. Then he showed her the money that he had brought for her, a hundred pounds in notes. He told her that he would maintain the child, he promised to get her father into a better job.

She made a scene and he said: "A woman like you is only for a man's convenience."

At that she sprang out of the car and ran to the top of the falls. She stood with the water round her ankles, shrieking that she was going to kill herself. Ray left her there and drove a few miles down the road. He intended to wait an hour and then go back to the falls to see whether Hester had come to her senses. Halfway there he met her struggling along the dusty road. She was carrying her coat. Her dress was tight on her swollen body and he saw with horror how close to her time she was.

She threw herself in front of the wheels. He tried to swerve but the mudguard caught her left leg; it was broken.

The last words she said to Ray were: "I'm going to that bitch of yours, I'll tell her . . ."

He stamped on her until she was silent. Then he drove back to the falls and threw her from the highest rock. She was still breathing when he threw her down.

He intended to give himself up at once but suddenly realized that he might be safe since she would drown in the pool and her broken bones would be attributed to her fall. If he had to, he could produce the letter in which she had threatened suicide.

He stayed at our house that night. When my father was asleep he came into my room and slept all night in my bed, for the first time. He imprinted his body on mine and for years afterwards in my loneliness I was able to recall the shape of him. He did not go away even when the maid brought in the coffee.

During the morning I heard my father quarrelling with him for the maid had told him that Ray had spent the night in my room. I went to my father.

"It's no use being angry, Pa. I'm going to have a baby."

He cried, over a thing like that. But he agreed to our marrying that week if we wanted to. Ray phoned through to Johannesburg, to make arrangements with the airline for our passages to Rome.

Hester Adraanse had crawled out of the water on to a rock. There she gave birth to her child before dying. That afternoon a herdboy saw the two corpses beneath the falls. Within an hour the police had arrested Ray.

The evidence against him was enough to hang him. There was only his word for it that he had met her with the sole intention of buying her off; he could have met her in Johannesburg; the hundred pounds might have been money for travelling expenses.

Before his trial, Mrs. Rottcher started a campaign for him in Perelkop and it flowed to all levels: Ray became almost a national hero. His fame as a sportsman . . . he was a rugby player . . . his wealth, his name, his unblemished record: all these were weighed against Hester Adraanse's light morals, the squalor of her family and her determination to ruin him.

Adraanse alone might have saved Ray. He was called on by the Prosecution to give an account of his daughter's seduction: it was the Defence that gained. There he stood in the witness box, wearing a bow tie, a shiny blue suit and the patent leather shoes, and told the Court that he had come on his daughter with Ray near the falls: another time he had found them together on a sofa in the big house when he went up to speak about the ploughing. He had said nothing to them but had gone away quietly: he was happy to see his daughter in the garden of Eden. He did not expect Ray to marry her: how could a man like Mr. Van Doorn have a father-in-law a bywoner, it never entered his head . . . Of course, if he found the treasure that had been promised to him. . . .

I could not sleep without dreaming of white thighs and secret dark hair. Between sleeping and waking, I rejoiced because Ray had killed for love of me.

He was found guilty with extenuating circumstances

and sentenced to fifteen years' imprisonment. We asked for permission to marry and it was granted soon after Ray began to serve his sentence.

My father had a horror of me. He had asked me not to marry Ray, out of pity for his two victims. He had offered to take me overseas and to care for my child.

After Bokkie was murdered, we drew together again. It was not only because I was ostracized in Perelkop. For the first time I could say that I pitied Hester Adraanse and her baby. I remembered them when I sat that afternoon beside poor little Bokkie's corpse.

CHAPTER 9

"They say Maarten will hang," Tante said to me as we sat in her kitchen.

I knew very well what she wanted me to answer; "Some people said my husband would hang, Tante."

A smirk touched her lips when I mentioned my husband. It was almost as though she said: Yes, he got off and look how he killed that girl, a White girl . . . "It's not as if Bokkie suffered and after all who can really blame a boy for losing his head when a Coloured tries to ruin his life?"

She was still stout three months after Maarten's arrest, but now the flesh was not holding to her bones. It sagged into jowls and pouches beneath chin and stomach and eyes. Her arms which had been as solid as legs of mutton had slackened and there were hollows on the under part of them. But her hair was still golden, incongruous above her ravaged face yet evidence of an innate resilience; I had the feeling that no matter what happened to Maarten she would recover and become with some modification the Tant Bertha

I had known. She was moulding clay on the kitchen table; a span of oxen pulling a Voortrekker wagon. Already she had put into the shoulders of the leaders swelling muscles that took the strain. "If we could trek away," she sighed, leaning back to look at the tiny figures. "I have no fear of Maarten hanging. Oh my dear God, I wouldn't be sitting here so quietly if I thought anything like that . . . but I'm wondering how long they will give him. He's twenty-three. Eight years? Pray God they don't give him fifteen years, that's a lifetime. You understand these things, Ilse, what do you think will happen?"

She got up to make coffee. The stove was still as bright as ever.

We had discussed the subject a hundred times but I said again: "Well, extenuating circumstances depend on Maarten proving definitely that it was not premeditated, Tante, that he acted on an uncontrollable impulse. He made no attempt to hide the body and he meant to give himself up. And I am ready to swear he had no motive, he was free of Bokkie . . . I don't think it will go hard with him."

"You know we got rid of Sipho," said Tante.

"Yes, he came to see me. He is living in the Storm valley."

"He still owes us money but Pieter thought it best to let him go. You never can tell with Kaffrs and the Greyling was his granddaughter when all is said and done. We're short of labour. I do nearly all the work myself, not the floors of course."

"Tante keeps the place beautiful."

"It will be better when Maarten is serving his sentence," she burst out passionately. "He will resign himself then and so will we. And he will have the comfort of knowing that I think of him night and day. His father and I are here, ready to help him when he comes out. If only he gets a light sentence. I'll be satisfied with eight years."

I said tentatively: "Have you thought it might be better if he has assessors rather than a jury? A jury is sometimes swayed by their feelings, the assessors go only on law."

"The lawyer is dead set against assessors. I wish we could have got somebody different from this little runt of a Schwegmann. But it's not everybody who wants to be mixed up in murder cases. Why shouldn't they call it manslaughter? He never meant to kill her. A Perelkop man would have known exactly how the case stood and what Maarten is like. The lawyer Corneels here, I always think he inspires such confidence. But we have to be satisfied with this little man from Pretoria. Everybody in Perelkop is against us. You and the minister are the only ones who ever come here now, and good Petrus Kotze. He rides out on his bike once a week. But Pieter is not so keen on him now. He wishes we had stuck to the Church like I always wanted him to."

She began to cry, with her hands hopelessly in her lap, and left the tears to splash unhindered into the crevices of her face. So she sat until the coffee with a noise of spitting boiled up through the spout on to the plate. Tante got up then and wiped the top of the stove, rubbing away at it until there remained only a slight discoloration on the satin of the plate.

We carried the coffee and some rusks to the church where Oubaas was working. He was alone, without even a child to help him but he had raised the walls to roof height since Maarten was arrested.

We took a long time over the coffee. We were cheerful suddenly. Oubaas had his arm round Tante's shoulders. He put his cheek against her hair.

The first crisis of their suffering had passed.

I thought it safe to speak of the child Diamant and as I was leaving I said to them: "Sipho came to see me the other day."

By then we were standing on the driveway where I had parked my car. Oubaas opened the door for me with a jerk.

"Did Sipho want a job?" asked Tante derisively.

"It was about the Greyling's child."

There was a bitter "So?" from the Oubaas but not a word from Tante. She only looked at me coldly.

"Sipho spoke about the money he owed you," I said.

"He'll find himself in gaol one of these days," said the Oubaas. "He owes us nearly seventy pounds. We lent him money for lobolo for three of his sons and saw no risk since they were all working here."

"Sipho talked about the Greyling's lobolo to me." Once the word was out, I was sorry I had said it. The Oubaas was so pale that I thought he would faint and Tante looked at me from a deepening well of hatred.

"Sipho had better look out," said the Oubaas. "If I get my hands on him . . ."

"In the meantime there is the child at Banghoek. Sipho said that he took no responsibility for her, the responsibility is yours. Mrs. Rottcher has stirred up the Child Welfare, she is on the committee you know, and they have been writing to me. There is an approved woman in Perelkop who will act as temporary foster-mother. It costs five shillings a week. I could send her there. The Welfare wants to arrange an adoption but they would like the signature of the guardian first. That was why I sent for Sipho. But he says Maarten is her guardian, since he has his lobolo. . . ."

"We'll take Sipho to Court for the money he owes us," said Tante. "And Maarten has no money now. All that there was has been used up for the lawyers. Lobolo! Such a word would come from you, Ilse Van Doorn. You who betrayed my son . . . Judas Iscariot."

Oubaas said, "Sorry. Hi shame, Bertha."

I felt bruised as though I had thrown myself against a rock.

I sent the child to Perelkop, to the Coloured woman Nessie Huurman. She was already foster-mother to four other small Coloureds. I was expecting to pay the five shillings out of my own pocket but at the end of the month the Oubaas called and left a pound on the sideboard. Tante had sent me a bottle of her orange preserve as a peace-offering.

"She begs you to visit her again," said the Oubaas, "only say nothing about the child or that I have paid for its keep. She refuses to acknowledge its existence."

The house at Diamant was still clean and there were flowers in the vases and pretty doilies out.

"I wanted to talk to you about Maarten's case," Tante said, kissing me. "We were in Pretoria yesterday to see the lawyer. I dislike him more and more. He wants to see you some time this month and discuss your evidence. I told him that people are against Maarten and shouldn't he rather have assessors? Ilse, he says no, Maarten was already a criminal before he . . . before he hurt the Greyling . . . he says there is a motive, they will make out that Maarten was covering up his first crime, it was a crime for him to have connection with that devil of a girl. He was already liable for prison. You see? It's dangerous, the lawyer says."

She had taken a few handfuls of green peas on to her lap and began to shell them: there was a curry cooking on the stove. She cracked the pods deftly between finger and thumb, then ran her nail behind the peas, shooting them into an enamel mug, all in one movement. She did this monotonously and it seemed to soothe her; that and the talking.

Tante and the Oubaas were at the hotel when the sergeant of police telephoned to tell them that Maarten had been arrested. Tante took the call because of the Oubaas's deafness. It was a bright morning and Tante was longing to get out of the stuffy hotel into the streets: she felt like walking for miles. When the Native called her to the telephone she thought it was Maarten or one of the Bruggemanns who wanted to speak to her for nobody else knew what hotel they were staying at.

"This is Sergeant Marais of Perelkop."

She thought Bruggemann was playing a joke on her.

"Go on with you," she shouted over the telephone and she held the receiver away from her while she laughed.

When she listened again the voice was saying: "Your son was arrested at 4 a.m. this morning on a charge of murdering a Coloured woman known as Bokkie Sipho, and contravening the Immorality Act. He is in hospital at present with a slight stab wound . . ." She knew then that this was not a joke. The laughter that had been bubbling in her throat was transformed into a howl of grief. The manager of the hotel took the telephone from her and spoke to Marais.

The Oubaas had not heard her cries. He was in their room reading the newspaper and he had not yet put in his hearing aid. A Native waiter came and shook him by the arm. Oubaas was furious and sprang up, brushing the sleeve of his coat where the Native had clutched him. That was how Tant Bertha saw him as she came into the room propelled by the frenzied manager.

There ensued greater confusion because the Oubaas could not find his hearing aid. He knew something terrible had happened but he could not follow what his wife or the manager said while he was hunting for the hearing aid.

"Stand still, stand still, read our lips," Tante was shrieking and the manager all the time dancing about in anguish as he begged her to hush for the corridors were full of people. He wanted them out of the hotel as soon as possible. He was snarling at them in the end and called them scum for having got mixed up with Coloureds. Tante managed to get on the side of the Oubaas's good ear and bellowed down it. The manager threatened them with the police if they did not leave his hotel at once. He even helped them to pack and himself ran out with their suitcase to the lorry though there were dozens of servants standing around.

The Oubaas was fairly calm. He knew that something had happened to Maarten but he had caught only a few words and thought that Maarten having been stabbed by a Coloured was all there was to the affair.

He said: "We'll get Ella and race back to Jakkalspan, I suppose he's in the hospital there. Bertha, there's one thing I've been against all my life and that is Coloureds carrying knives. My God, if there is a vital organ pierced . . . Those streets in Perelkop are a den of thieves, I've said to Martie: Whatever you do, walk in the middle of the street, then you can see what is coming at you. . . ." Tant Bertha looked at him in terror. She felt herself to be on the verge of a faint, sweat poured from her suddenly: to have to tell him again what had happened to Maarten seemed beyond her power. She wished him dead at the wheel still believing the fantasy created for him by his deafness.

They were only a block away from the Bruggemanns' house and still she could not speak. Her thighs had stuck together, she was sweating so heavily, she told me that morning; sweat ran from the tips of her fingers and formed little pools on the seat. At last she brought herself to touch her husband's arm.

"Stop the lorry," she yelled into his good ear.

He drew in at the kerb, thinking she was sick for he had noticed the sweat on her. She opened the suitcase which was on the seat between them. "Do you need aspirins, love?" he said. She went through the suitcase carefully, searching for his hearing aid. It was like looking for a whip to thrash him. She found the aid in his dressing-gown pocket and gave it to him. He adjusted it.

"When you are looking for one thing you often find another," said the Oubaas. "How I hunted for this damn hearing aid in the hotel."

Tante did not bother to pack the things into the

suitcase again but left them lying about on the seat. She reached over and took his hand.

She said: "Beloved. My treasure. God will help us. You haven't grasped what has happened."

"Well, what is it, woman?"

"You misunderstood," said Tante, crying. "Martie has been arrested for murdering the Greyling. He is not at Jakkalspan at all but at Perelkop."

"Is that so?" said the Oubaas with imbecile politeness, holding tenderly on to the lobe of his ear where the tiny cord of the hearing aid rested. He went on: "Well, I suppose we must still go and fetch Ella. She will want to help. Say nothing about the immorality yet."

They drove on. Tante stopped sweating. She prayed in thankfulness. She had thought Oubaas would collapse with shock but he was taut and suddenly seemed younger; he was holding his muscles together with every ounce of his power.

Neither Ella nor her sister-in-law was dressed although Bruggemann had left for work. Cissie came into the lounge in her housecoat but Ella was scrambling into a dress.

"Afraid of making a bad impression on her future in-laws," Cissie laughed. "It just happened that today we were lazy. Baba, tell Tante we are lazy."

Neither Tante nor the Oubaas so much as glanced at the baby in her arms.

"May we talk to Ella alone?" Tante said because she did not have the courage to tell this young woman, smiling as she was at them, and so respectful, that their son had been arrested on a charge of murdering a Coloured woman.

Ella came in then, almost dancing, and with her hair frothing up to meet the sunlight that poured into the room. My time, she looked pretty, said Tante wistfully: she had been so happy since receiving Maarten's telephone call.

Cissie went out. Tante could only sit staring at Ella who realizing now that something was wrong crept to her side and knelt there. Oubaas spoke. He said that Martie was innocent, there would be a case against the Government for wrongful arrest, or they would find that the girl was killed while trying to steal.

While he talked, Ella got to her feet. Oubaas stood up too but she did not look at him. She looked at Tante with a piercing, bird-like look. The little nose was pointed downwards like a beak that would peck at Tante.

"You are wrong," Ella said. "Maarten has been carrying on with that girl."

"Don't dare say that," cried Tante and she stood up to defend herself against the bright-eyed girl.

"I dare say it, I dare," Ella screamed. "I know the girl . . . that one who served at the table and afterwards came into my room. He has had that girl. I know it as surely as I stand here. He was cold towards me." She began to pant.

Tante raised her fist as though to strike Ella who now ran out of the room into her sister-in-law's arms. They heard her gasping in an attack of breathlessness. Tante did not go forward to help though the Oubaas urged her to go to the girl and try and win her over.

Tante could not move. She felt herself constricted as if by ice and her very brain was cold in her head.

"Let us go," said the Oubaas.

Cissie Bruggemann came into the passage when they were leaving. She was stiff with them as though they were strangers to her.

There was a telephone box in the corner. Tante put a call through to me. She listened quietly enough while I told her something of what had happened, until I mentioned the baby. Then I heard her draw in her breath as if she had been stabbed by an exquisite pain.

In the street she said to the Oubaas: "There is a child. Maarten has fathered a Coloured child."

"Then God has forsaken us."

"You knew about Martie and the Greyling," Tante accused him.

"I only had a vague idea."

They started on the road to Perelkop.

"When I think of Cissie Bruggemann and that Ella," said Tante. "But one could stand being treated like that . . . no matter. It's nothing. But I'm afraid, Pieter. When it comes to Court . . . if he killed her, will they hang him, Pieter?"

"Lightning and thunder, don't talk like that," said the Oubaas. "Hold your mouth, will you, you vile bitch."

Tante cried out in rage against him: "Why did you not tell me that you had this idea about him and the Greyling?"

"What for? I did the only thing I could. I sent him to Plat Anna to cool him off when I noticed the signs."

"You did that? My poor boy."

"I did the best for him. Maarten would never pray with me. I handled the problem in a material way. I told him to leave decent girls alone unless he married one and if he must go to anybody let it be to Plat Anna until he did get married."

"Plat Anna. My God, my God," Tante moaned.

"Was it better what he did, going to the Coloured?" Oubaas asked.

He was crying. The lorry swerved all over the road for a while.

If they could have stopped, said Tante, if they could have found some quiet place in which to call on God for help, if they could have sat in a moment of silence while the bitter sea washed over them . . . but Oubaas drove on and on. They did pray. It took them six hours to get to Perelkop and they did not speak again except to pray or say a psalm.

At the Perelkop garage, Oubaas said to her: "Make yourself look respectable, old treasure," and himself began to pull back the fine golden hair into its bun. He took a handkerchief from the pile of clothing on the seat to wipe her face.

"We must tidy up," he muttered. "We mustn't leave it like this. Nobody must get the impression of laxness, you understand. Tidy it up, beloved."

So Tante had to sit there and fold away the garments while Oubaas tightened the tarpaulin and got a boy to wipe away the dust on the wheels. As he smoothed his own hair, he lamented the carelessness of their lives; those vagabond years on the diggings, the wild evangelist, the church he had never completed for God.

"We should have gone to church regularly, we should have lived conventional lives. Somewhere we sowed the seeds of wickedness in him."

"No," said Tante. "You hear even of ministers taking Native girls. It is like lightning, it can miss one house and strike the next and you can never say why it is so."

They were allowed to see Maarten in the ward but little was said then except to reassure him that they would stand by him. Their next meeting was in a cell-like room where the bars on the windows cast shadows on the concrete outside. Tante took his head on her breast. There remained deep within her some of the ice that had formed at the Bruggemanns' place that first morning; a small cold spot that was lapped around and eaten at by the warmth of her feelings yet did not vanish though she held her son closer and closer until they were both bruised.

"Mother, she was waiting for me at the place where we used to meet. She had been listening for my footsteps on the path. I went there before she called me. I think I would have been disappointed if I had not found her there. I stayed a while with her. Kiss me goodbye too, Martie, she said: I had kissed the baby. She was crying. I kissed her. Then it happened between us again. I said, Come near me again you bastard, and I'll do this to you. I choked her, to frighten her. When I let go, she said: Basie, you may think you have got away from me but you never will. Even when I am married . . . if I do marry Luke . . . you will come running after me as you have always done and that fair one whom you are marrying to please your father will be left lying alone in her bed. You are here now with me instead of with her. Why didn't you just post the money? I choked her until she was dead."

143

"'But why?" Tante wept. "Why didn't you just kick her aside and go?"

"Because what she said is true. After I broke with her I used to dream about her and I looked at other Coloured girls but I did not feel like them, nor Kaffir women, nor White women. I wanted only her. Usually when I sat up with Ella, nothing came; it was just as if she were made of wood."

"She bewitched you. Oh God, you let her bewitch my son."

"I should have killed myself. I meant to. I went to the house and got in at the kitchen window . . . you know how I can open it with a pocket knife. I got my gun. I was going to kill the baby and myself. But I couldn't shoot. I just walked on and on until I came to Bokkie's place in the valley. I went over the fence of a kraal and milked a goat to give the baby some milk. We both slept. I was going to kill myself as soon as somebody came. When I woke up I thought it was Bokkie who had come, I thought she had brought herself to life to save us: Bokkie would have cut off her right arm for me. But it was Luke who was in the room."

That day Maarten confessed to the murder of the Greyling.

The Greyling's ghost haunted Perelkop. Coloured women spent days decorating her grave with pieces of glass and shells. There were always fresh flowers in an expensive terrazzo urn that perched on top of the mound. Even White women driving past the non-European cemetery would stop for a moment to point out where the Greyling lay.

Presents poured in on Diamant who was still in

Nessie Huurman's care. After the preparatory examination thirty people offered to adopt her. Nothing came of these offers because the Child Welfare authorities decided to wait until the publicity of Maarten's case had abated.

CHAPTER 10

At Maarten's trial a subtle tangle of emotion and statutes enmeshed the counsel of the Defence. His appeal to the jury was that Maarten was driven by fear of losing his fiancée and had been the victim of an uncontrollable impulse; but this was bound up with the fact that Maarten was liable to imprisonment for contravening the Immorality Act before he killed Bokkie. The Prosecution argued that Maarten was concerned not with the fear of losing his fiancée but with a fear of the police.

I gave evidence that he had not attempted to injure Bokkie after I found them together or after her baby was born: the Prosecutor pointed out that if Bokkie had been murdered then, suspicion must have fallen directly on Maarten. As it was, Luke provided an alternative suspect as soon as Bokkie jilted him.

So it went on. The Defence brought two witnesses to prove that Bokkie was not serious in her intention of jilting Luke but had meant to follow her ordinary routine on the following day and meet him: she had arranged for the girl to look after her baby and with the driver of a market lorry to give her a lift to Perel-kop. These witnesses were demolished: Bokkie had not had time to see them and cancel her arrangements before she went to meet Maarten.

As to Maarten's being in love, why had he not gone to Bloemfontein to seal his engagement? He could just as well have posted the money to me. Most men did not telephone a proposal. It looked as though he were not in love but using his fiancée to get him out of an entanglement with a Coloured girl.

Even his love for his child did not tell wholly in his favour for it was argued that he had risked fathering another Coloured child who might have been brought up among Black relations.

The judge found that Maarten had killed because he had contravened the Immorality Act: his motive was to hide this crime.

I sat with Tante and the Oubaas while the jury retired. We could hear the sound of a piano-accordion; throughout the trial those who could not get into the courtroom had crowded on to the pavements outside. There were men throwing dice and like bookmakers calling the odds on the verdict. Somebody had drawn in chalk on the pavement a crude gallows with a hanging man.

Maarten's name was loathed, not only by the Coloureds but by the Blacks who also claimed Bokkie; and by the Whites who saw themselves betrayed through a supporter of Apartheid. The country clamoured for his blood.

While we waited there was a deep silence; the police had cleared the mob from the pavement. Then faintly, much farther away now, we heard the notes of the piano-accordion again.

The jury came in with a verdict of guilty. No extenuating circumstances were found and Maarten was sentenced to death.

His appeal failed.

My father had got a friend who had gone overseas to lend the Delports a furnished flat in Pretoria and they stayed there until Maarten was executed. On his last morning which was in February, the lawyer was still trying for a reprieve and we sat from before dawn waiting for the telephone to ring.

The telephone was silent. Maarten's time came. The minister, Kotze and I prayed but Tante and the Oubaas could not pray or even turn towards each other: it looked as though God had forsaken them. The Oubaas at last began a psalm: Hear my cry, O God, attend unto my prayer . . . but Tante screamed: "They are killing my child," and ran from the flat on to the road. She pounded along, signalling to cars; they all passed her, some with derisive hooting, for a bus stood waiting at the terminus. Suddenly the street was quiet and we could hear the thud of Tante's feet on the pavement. She ran past the bus while the conductor and driver whistled and cat-called, and a solitary passenger leaned far out to watch: they must have thought that Tante was drunk. We found her at last on a park bench, crying distractedly, with a crowd of Natives and children watching her.

Maarten's body was recovered and Tante and the Oubaas went back to the farm to bury him. Tante put the coffin in her room and would let nobody in except the Oubaas. When I came she received me in the kitchen as usual. She had hastily tidied the place but I could see that a cloth had merely been dragged over the surface of things and that the floor had not been swept.

I had put on a black dress and brought some flowers because I thought the funeral was to be held that day. Tante sat looking at me stolidly.

"How are you off for labour?" I asked her for I had not seen a soul about the place.

"The servants have run away."

"Perhaps they will come back afterwards."

"After what, Ilse?"

I meant after the funeral and she knew that very well.

We sat there without a word. I was listening for the minister's car. She knew that too, for she said: "There's nobody coming here today."

"But Tante . . ."

"Ilse, go home. What do you want here? Have you come to look at my suffering? Your husband is safe. Yes, he killed and was not hanged. What did you do, Ilse? Did you bribe the jury? Is that what you did? My son did not kill his own child in the womb even though that child lay in a Coloured's womb. He did not send anybody in torture to her death. What did you do?" She began to shriek. "What did you do to save Ray Van Doorn?" I got up and tried to leave: she stood straddled in the doorway. "Yes, you must go, Ilse. Never come near me again. If it hadn't been for you, who would have known about that child? It could have stayed in the Storm valley hidden away as dozens are. There's many a respectable man walking about Perelkop at this minute with a half-caste safely tucked away. Where did the Greyling herself come from? Who was punished for that?"

"Only Bokkie herself, Tante. Try now to think of what was good in Maarten, that it all began because he wanted to save his child from suffering. . . ."

"Silence," she yelled.

Oubaas pushed her away from the door. She went close to the stove and sat there with her arms folded across her breast, a look of dreaming on her face.

Poor thing, she hoped that Maarten might still revive: in the doctor's book she had read a chapter on catalepsy. She had been trying all night to rub warmth back into his corpse and she was waiting for me to go so that she could continue.

The Oubaas put a stop to it. He sent for the evangelist and asked me if I could supply some boys to dig the grave: I had to send convicts.

I kept away.

During the funeral a dry thunderstorm raged. A tree in the plantation was struck.

The evangelist appeared suddenly at Banghoek on foot. He was chanting: "I am with thee, saith the Lord, to deliver thee . . ." He had left his bike kicking on the veld. He said he had seen the devil.

I took him in and gave him brandy.

He said: "A man appeared as I was riding along and put his hand on the tank of my motor-bike. He left a big mark on it that blistered the paint. He spoke to me: The day of judgment is at hand so prepare yourself. Then he loped beside me in the veld but I could not hear what he was saying because of the crashes of thunder. All of a sudden I found myself lying on the road with the bike beside me. There in the veld was the perfect print of a hoof burnt into the grass. Do you know what I think, Sister Van Doorn? I have been on the devil's business today."

"Might it not have been the lightning that burned the grass and your bike?"

"No. And rejoice that I have seen the devil, Sister. For if a man sees the devil then may the hour not come when he sees God?"

After the storm, he made me go back with him while he retrieved his motor-bike. The grass on the edge of the plantation had been burned and a great tree pulverized by the lightning. The evangelist was lucky to be alive.

He did not come to Diamant again.

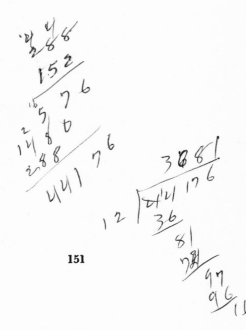

CHAPTER 11

An order had been signed for Ray's release in June. It was April when I first knew and Raymond was home for the Easter holidays.

When I told him, he said: "Did he have to work like the convicts do on the farms?"

"No. He was shut up in prison. He does upholstering."

"Sometimes I thought he might have to work like they do for Rottcher."

"It wasn't as bad as that. Only being shut in . . ."

"And being sorry for her and her baby." He looked at me with a question in his eyes.

"Yes. His face is lined like old Sipho's."

He said: "When he comes home I'll be good all the time."

Each morning I put a mark on the calendar. The difficulties facing us were for the future: now I was happy.

My position in the district had eased. After Maarten's execution fissures appeared in the solid wall of the Veld Guard. Maarten had identified himself so closely with Rottcher that some of his disgrace rubbed off on to the great man. Rottcher's enemies for the first time in years spoke out openly against him at the meetings of the Veld Guard: some women forced their sons to resign.

Mrs. Rottcher came to see me again. She hinted now that what I had done might be attributed to the sinister influence of poor Tant Bertha; and of that renegade, my father.

"We'll see a change at Banghoek when Ray comes home," she said.

She would find out for herself that she did not know the Ray Van Doorn who was coming back in June. He had listened with sardonic enjoyment when I told him of the activities of the Veld Guard: Maarten Delport's fall had not come as a surprise to him.

I tried often to see Tant Bertha but her door was closed to me; her desolation chilled me.

Then one day a herdboy brought a message from her: Would I come?

The Oubaas was putting a roof on the church, bright sheets of corrugated iron. "It's slow," he said, "It takes me days to get a sheet in position. The trouble is I'm no builder."

He waved me on to the house. I pushed open the kitchen door. A chunk of wood fell off as I touched it; the white ants had won the long battle.

Tante must have had a servant for the floors were brightly polished and there was no dust on the furniture. Only the stove was rather dull and I saw on the arm of a chair a drying peach pip: Tante had not been in here for a long time.

"Have you come, Ilse?" she said from the bedroom.
She was lying in the big bed that Raymond and I
had shared. The curtains were pulled across the window.

"Will you open the curtains, please?"

She tried to raise herself on to her elbow but fell
again to lie as I had found her; on her back with her
eyes closed. She must have caught a glimpse of the veld
for she said: "Everything is green. I've heard the rain
drumming on the roof for nights now. You miss that
when you have tiles on the roof. I like the sound of
rain on a tin room." She opened her eyes and held
out her hand to me. "Sorry, Ilse. Sorry for all I said."

"Ag, don't say sorry, Tante."

"Pieter says your husband is coming back."

"Yes."

"Happy now?"

"Yes, Tante."

"Won't he mind you coming here?"

"No. There's nothing like that left in him."

"Ilse, would you make me a little arrowroot with a
spoonful of honey in it. If there's none, some cornflour
porridge would do."

Her hair had turned white. She was no longer stout.
The flesh had fallen into the hollows made by her
bones on her face and chest, and hung in cords on her
arms. She was like a piece of veld that has been over-
grazed and burnt too often and has fallen into a ruin
of dongas and parched grass.

She struggled up to eat the arrowroot, forcing it
down her throat even when she heaved over it.

"And now a cloth and soap and some warm water,

154

if you would," she said when she had finished. "A woman is a comfort. A man . . . Fatherland!"

She washed and got out of bed. At the mirror she combed her hair and made it up in a bun. She stared at herself.

"My hair so white! I'll have to get used to it." She sat by the window. "That child?"

"She is still with Nessie Huurman in Perelkop."

"I'm going there this afternoon."

"To see her?"

"It's Maarten's child. I'm going to fetch her. Pieter and I will look after her."

"Tante, they won't allow it."

She took her best dress out of the wardrobe and a pair of black stockings from the drawer. She dressed carefully, brushing off the pieces of fluff that clung to her skirt. She was gaunt and old in the black dress which hung on her like another skin.

"Where is Nessie Huurman's place?"

"Near Mahomedy's. But I'll drive you there, Tante."

"I couldn't. What would your husband say?"

"I told you: nothing like that would worry him."

"Then thank you, Ilse."

"But what about the Oubaas?"

"We've come step by step to this together, Ilse, though I think it was easier for him. Pieter does not love the world as much as I do. He was going to take me to Perelkop himself but he grudges the time. The work on the church is so precious to him, he wants it all covered over." She pinned on her hat. "You know, Martie loved the Greyling. He tried to tell me but I would not listen.

"Ilse, when I went in to see him, I held him in my

arms. I held his head against my breasts. We stood like that and the thought came to me from some cold spot within me: So his head lay on those dark breasts. I saw him upon the Greyling. I saw him send our seed into her womb to make a bastard child . . . and I don't know if I released him, or if I ceased to hold him tightly, but he knew that I had drawn away from him. It was for one little moment but he got frightened. He had no hope from that day; it was that day he confessed to the police."

"You know that nothing could have saved him, Tante. They condemned him on a point of law."

"Perhaps so. But never again did he speak to me about Greyie or the child, not even when I saw him for the last time. All he could say was that he was sorry. She was flesh of his flesh . . . And the Lord God planted a garden eastward in Eden . . . but we have made a blasphemy of it. I said to Pieter, If you want to write anything on his tombstone put: I was the beloved of Bokkie Sipho.

"Lying here day after day, night after night, I've thought about Maarten's life from his first hour to his last: from first to last we taught him to love his Whiteness above everything else, above Christ, above his own need of a woman . . . we put him in hell; not only Rottcher but all of us who brought him up. They looked for his motive for killing her: nobody knew that he considered it a worse sin to love her than to take her as if she were a whore.

"I've torn a cancer out of myself, Ilse . . . no, I've died and come to life. . . . But now I can say: Bokkie's child is ours."

We went to Perelkop. There were five children toddling about on the stoep of Nessie's house.

"Which one is my grandchild?" Tant Bertha asked.

I put my hand on Diamant. Tant Bertha held the child from her by the arms and looked at her.

"I am seeking Maarten."

Diamant was the colour of old parchment. Her hair still had a golden tinge. She had her mother's strange eyes lying like pools of water in her face.

"She is more like Bokkie," I said.

"Maarten's hands though . . . those fingers. Wait." She put her finger between the child's teeth and opened her mouth. "The tongue is caught, like Maarten's was, like my own." And she rolled her tongue back to show the white tendon holding it down.

Nessie had come out.

"I am taking my grandchild," Tante said. "Is there something owing?"

"Madam, you can't take her. The Welfare lady is coming tomorrow and bringing a couple who are going to adopt her. They have been after her for months but Mrs. Rottcher always said the publicity should be over before the child is adopted . . . some people just want limelight."

"Is there anything owing?" Tante asked, taking a hold on Diamant.

"Only the pound for last month," said Nessie. "You understand, madam, if you take her, I'll report it straight to the Welfare."

Nessie must have rung up as we left the house with the child: Mrs. Rottcher was waiting at Diamant when we got there. Her shadow fell like a whiplash on Tante.

"You had no right to take that child away, Mrs.

Delport," she said. "She is under the Welfare. I'll take her back now."

"No," said Tante. "Pieter and I are her guardians. Ask Sipho. We paid lobolo."

"Sis. How can you talk so? But you won't get very far. The Welfare has the authority to dispose of the child. And your son wished her to be adopted into the Coloured community."

"We're keeping her," said Tante but faintly for she was afraid of Mrs. Rottcher who was speaking calmly as though she were at a committee meeting.

Tante went inside with the child.

"I give you until tomorrow morning at nine o'clock," said Mrs. Rottcher to the Oubaas. "The Lord knows we want no more publicity of this sort in Perelkop. But if that child is not handed over to me by nine, I'll call a meeting and we'll get a warrant. But you would think your son's wishes would count for something . . . at least he saw what was the right thing to do."

"If he had known we would take her . . ." muttered the Oubaas, shrivelled and humble before her.

"Until nine o'clock," warned Mrs. Rottcher and to me: "Your husband will hear about this."

In the bedroom Tante had gathered together her jewellery on the bed. The child was asleep there in a nest of pillows.

"We'll hide, Ilse."

"Where will you go?"

"Pieter will find a place for us to creep into. Say farewell now. But take this. I made it when you told me about the garden of Eden. Before that I had never made naked figures."

The model was of a man and a woman, more roughly done than Tante's other work: she must have moulded it in secret.

During the night she and the Oubaas fled with the child. I do not know where they went for I have not heard from them since but I think they went to Bechuanaland: the Oubaas spent his childhood there.

A few days after their flight as I was driving to Perel-kop I heard the sound of hammering at Diamant. I thought the Delports had come back so I stopped the car and went over to the church: the house was locked.

It was not the Oubaas on the roof, it was Sipho.

He told me that when it was all worked out, he owed a month's work on Diamant so he was filling in the time nailing on the last of the corrugated sheets to the roof since the Oubaas had not had time to do this.

He finished the little church for the Oubaas. There is no glass in the window-frames. The winds blow through the church, the sun and moon shine in and a heavy rain will wet all except a portion near the top. If you look in you might think there was a carpet there so thickly is it covered with weeds.

Maarten is buried at the far end of the church where no rain falls. Oubaas had bought a tombstone but had not put it up for the mound was still high when he left. The stone lies in the middle of the church. Leaning in through the window on a sunny day, you can see the lines Oubaas had inscribed on it: . . . I will abide in thy tabernacle for ever: I will trust in the covert of thy wings.

159